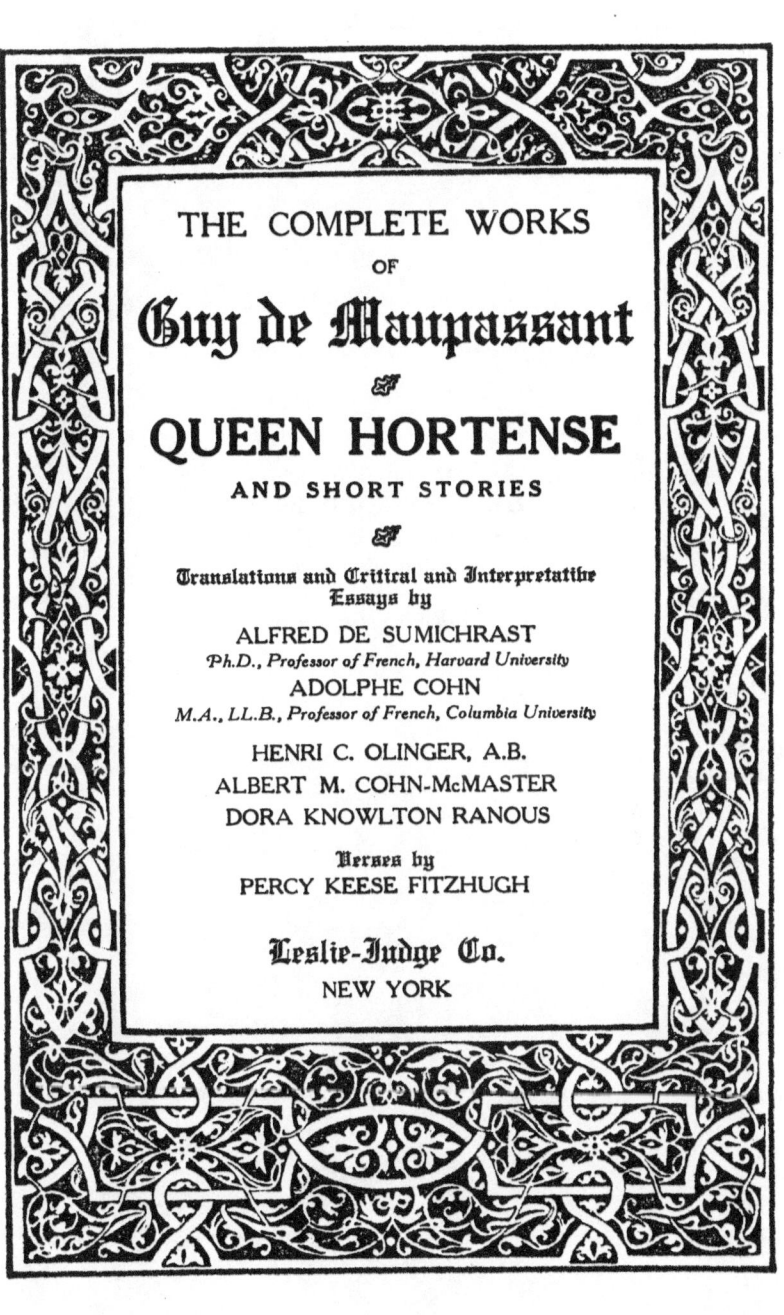

# THE COMPLETE WORKS

OF

# Guy de Maupassant

&

# QUEEN HORTENSE

AND SHORT STORIES

&

Translations and Critical and Interpretative
Essays by

ALFRED DE SUMICHRAST
*Ph.D., Professor of French, Harvard University*

ADOLPHE COHN
*M.A., LL.B., Professor of French, Columbia University*

HENRI C. OLINGER, A.B.
ALBERT M. COHN-McMASTER
DORA KNOWLTON RANOUS

Verses by
PERCY KEESE FITZHUGH

Leslie-Judge Co.
NEW YORK

# Contents

# Queen Hortense

IN Argenteuil she was called Queen Hortense. No one knew why. Perhaps it was because she had a commanding tone of voice; perhaps because she was tall, bony, imperious; perhaps because she governed a kingdom of servants, chickens, dogs, cats, canaries, parrots, and all the animals so dear to an old maid's heart. But she did not spoil these familiar friends; she had for them none of those endearing names nor of the foolish tenderness which women seem to lavish on the soft fur of a purring cat. She governed these beasts with authority; she reigned.

She was indeed an old maid—one of those old maids with a harsh voice and angular motions, whose very soul seems to be hard. She never would stand contradiction, impudence, hesitation, indifference, laziness, nor fatigue. She had never been heard to complain, to regret anything, to envy anyone. She would say: " Everyone has his share," with the conviction of a fatalist. She did not go to church, she had no use for priests, she hardly believed in God, calling all religious things '' weeper's wares.''

For thirty years she had lived in her little house, with its tiny garden running along the street; she had never changed her habits, only changing her servants pitilessly, as soon as they reached twenty-one years of age.

When her dogs, cats and birds would die of old age or from an accident, she would replace them without tears and without regret; with a little spade, she would bury the dead animal in a strip of ground, throwing a few shovelfuls of earth over it and stamping it down with her feet, in an indifferent manner.

She had a few friends in town, families of clerks who went to Paris every day. Once in a while she would be invited out, in the evening, for tea. She would inevitably fall asleep, and she would have to be awakened when it was time for her to go home. She never allowed anyone to accompany her, fearing neither light nor darkness. She did not appear to like children.

She kept herself busy doing countless male tasks —carpentering, gardening, sawing or chopping wood, even laying bricks when it was necessary.

She had relatives who came to see her twice a year, the Cimmes and the Colombels, her two sisters having married, one of them a florist and the other a retired merchant. The Cimmes had no children; the Colombels had three: Henri, Pauline, and Joseph. Henri was twenty, Pauline seventeen, and Joseph only three.

There was no love lost between the old maid and her relatives.

In the spring of the year 1882, Queen Hortense suddenly fell sick. The neighbors called in a physician, whom she immediately drove out. A priest then having presented himself, she jumped out of bed, half naked, to throw him out of the house.

The young servant, in despair, was brewing her some tea.

After lying in bed for three days, the situation appeared so serious that the barrel-maker, who lived on the right side of her, on advice from the doctor, who had forcibly returned to the house, took it upon himself to call together the two families.

They arrived by the same train, towards ten in the morning, the Colombels bringing little Joseph with them.

When they got to the garden gate, they saw the servant, seated in the chair against the wall, crying.

The dog was sleeping on the door mat in the broiling sun; two cats, which looked as though they might be dead, were stretched out in front of two windows, their eyes closed, their paws and tails spread out at full length.

A big, clucking hen was parading through the garden with a whole regiment of yellow, downy chicks; and a big cage hanging from the wall, covered with pimpernel, contained a kingdom of birds; which were chirping away in the warmth of this beautiful spring morning.

In another cage, shaped like a châlet, two inseparable partners were perched, motionless, side by side on their little swing.

M. Cimme, a fat, puffing person, who always entered first everywhere, pushing everyone else aside, whether man or woman, when it was necessary, asked:

"Well, Céleste, aren't things going well?"

The little servant moaned through her tears:

"She doesn't even recognize me any more. The doctor says it's the end."

Everybody looked around.

Madame Cimme and Madame Colombel then embraced each other, without saying a word. They looked very much alike, having always worn their hair drawn tight over their scalps and loud red cashmere shawls.

Cimme turned to his brother-in-law, a pale, sallow-complexioned, thin man, wasted by stomach complaints and who limped badly, and said in a serious tone of voice:

"Gad! It was high time."

But no one dared to enter the dying woman's room on the ground floor. Even Cimme made way for the others. Colombel was the first to make up his mind, and, swaying from side to side like the mast of a ship, the iron ferrule of his cane resounding against the floor, he entered.

The two women were the next to venture, and M. Cimme closed the procession.

Little Joseph had remained outside, pleased at the sight of the dog.

A ray of sunlight seemed to cut the bed in two, shining just on the hands, which were moving nervously, continually opening and closing. The fingers were twitching as though moved by some thought, as though trying to point out a meaning or idea, as

though obeying the dictates of a will. The rest of
the body lay motionless under the sheets. The angular frame showed not a single movement. The
eyes remained closed.

The family spread out in a semi-circle and, without a word, they began to watch the contracted chest
and the short, gasping breathing. The little servant
had followed them and was still crying.

At last, Cimme asked:

" Exactly what did the doctor say? "

The girl stammered:

" He said to leave her alone, that nothing more
could be done for her."

But suddenly the old woman's lips began to move.
She seemed to be uttering silent words, words hidden
in the head of this dying being, and her hands quickened their peculiar movements.

Then she began to speak in a thin, high voice,
which no one had ever heard, a voice which seemed
to come from the distance, perhaps from the depths
of this heart which had always been closed.

Cimme, finding this scene painful, was walking
around on tiptoe. Colombel, whose crippled leg was
growing tired, sat down.

The two women remained standing.

Queen Hortense was now babbling away, and no
one could understand a word. She was pronouncing
names, many names, calling imaginary people.

" Come here, Philippe, kiss your mother. Tell
me, child, do you love your mamma? You, Rose, take
care of your little sister while I am away. And don't
leave her alone. Don't play with matches! "

She stopped for a while, then, in a louder voice,
as though she were calling someone: " Henriette! "
then waited a moment, and continued:

" Tell your father that I wish to speak to him before he goes to business." And suddenly: " I am not feeling very well to-day, darling; promise not to come home late. Tell your employer that I am sick. You know, it isn't safe to leave the children alone when I am in bed. For dinner I will fix you up a nice dish of rice. The little ones like that very much. Won't Claire be happy! "

And she broke out in a happy, joyous laugh, such as they had never heard: " Look, Jean, how funny he looks! He has smeared jam all over his face, the little pig! Look, sweetheart, look, isn't he funny? "

Colombel, who was continually lifting his tired leg from place to place, muttered:

" She is dreaming that she has children and a husband; it is the beginning of the death agony."

The two sisters had not yet moved, surprised, astounded.

The little maid exclaimed:

" You must take off your shawls and your hats! Would you like to go into the parlor? "

They went out without having said a word. And Colombel followed them, limping, once more leaving the dying woman alone.

When they were relieved of their traveling garments, the women finally sat down. Then one of the cats left its window, stretched, jumped into the room, up on Madame Cimme's knees, who began to pet it.

In the next room could be heard the voice of the dying woman, living, in this last hour, the life for which she had doubtless hoped, living her dreams themselves, when all was over for her.

Cimme, in the garden, was playing with little Joseph and the dog, enjoying himself in the wholehearted manner of a man from the fields, having completely forgotten the dying woman.

But suddenly he entered the house, and, speaking to the girl:

" I say, my girl, are we not going to have luncheon? What do you ladies wish to eat? "

They finally agreed on an omelet, a piece of steak with new potatoes, cheese and coffee.

As Madame Colombel was fumbling in her pocket for her purse, Cimme stopped her, and, turning to the maid: " Have you got any money? "

She answered:

" Yes, Monsieur."

" How much? "

" Fifteen francs."

" That's enough. Hasten, my girl, because I am beginning to get very hungry."

Madame Cimme, looking over the climbing vines bathed in sunlight, and at the two turtle-doves on the roof opposite, said in an annoyed tone of voice:

" What a pity to have had to come for such a sad occasion. It is so nice in the country to-day."

Her sister sighed without answering, and Colombel mumbled, moved perhaps by the walk ahead of him:

" My leg certainly is bothering me to-day."

Little Joseph and the dog were making a terrible noise; one was shrieking with pleasure, the other was barking wildly. They were playing hide-and-seek around the three flower beds, running after each other like mad.

The dying woman continued to call her children, talking with each one, imagining that she was dressing them, fondling them, teaching them how to read:

" Come on! Simon, repeat: A, B, C, D. You are

not paying attention, listen—D, D, D; do you hear me? Now repeat——''

Cimme exclaimed: " Funny what people say when in that condition.''

Madame Colombel then asked:

" Wouldn't it be better if we were to return to her? ''

But Cimme dissuaded her from the idea:

" What's the use? You can't change anything! We are just as comfortable here.''

Nobody insisted. Madame Cimme observed the green birds, called inseparable. In a few words she praised this singular faithfulness, and blamed the men for not imitating these animals. Cimme began to laugh, looked at his wife and began to hum in a bantering way: " Tra-la-la, tra-la-la,'' as though to cast a good deal of doubt on his own, Cimme's, faithfulness.

Colombel was suffering from cramps, and was rapping the floor with his cane.

The other cat, its tail pointing upright to the sky, now came in.

They sat down to luncheon at one o'clock.

As soon as he had tasted the wine, Colombel, for whom only the best of Bordeaux had been prescribed, called the servant back:

" I say, my girl, is this the best stuff that you have in the cellar? ''

" No, Monsieur; there is some better wine, which was only brought out when you came.''

" Well, bring us three bottles of it! ''

They tasted the wine and found it excellent, not because it was of a remarkable vintage, but because it had been in the cellar fifteen years. Cimme declared:

" That is regular invalid's wine! "

Colombel, filled with an ardent desire to gain possession of this Bordeaux, once more questioned the girl:

" How much of it is left? "

" Oh! Almost all, Monsieur; Mamz'elle never touched it. It's in the bottom stack."

Then he turned to his brother-in-law:

" If you wish, Cimme, I would be willing to exchange something else for this wine; it suits my stomach marvelously."

The chicken had now appeared with its regiment of young ones; the two women were enjoying themselves throwing crumbs to them.

Joseph and the dog, who had eaten enough, were sent back to the garden.

Queen Hortense was still talking, but in a low, hushed voice, so that the words could no longer be distinguished.

When they had finished their coffee, all went in to observe the condition of the sick woman. She seemed calm.

They went outside again and seated themselves in a circle in the garden, in order to complete their digestion.

Suddenly the dog, who was carrying something in his mouth, began to run around the chairs at full speed. The child was chasing him wildly. Both disappeared into the house.

Cimme fell asleep, his well-rounded stomach bathed in the glow of the shining sun.

The dying woman once more began to talk in a loud voice. Then suddenly she shrieked.

The two women and Colombel rushed in to see what was the matter. Cimme, awakened, did not budge, because he did not wish to witness such a scene.

She was sitting up, with haggard eyes. Her dog, in order to escape being pursued by little Joseph, had jumped up on the bed, run over the sick woman, an entrenched behind the pillow, was looking down at his playmate with snapping eyes, ready to jump down and begin the game again. He was holding in his mouth one of his mistress's slippers, which he had torn to pieces, and with which he had been playing for the last hour.

The child, frightened by this woman who had suddenly risen in front of him, stood motionless before the bed.

The hen had also come in, and frightened by the noise, had jumped up on a chair; and was wildly calling her chicks, who were chirping, bewildered, around the four legs of the chair.

Queen Hortense was shrieking:

" No, no, I don't want to die, I don't want to! I don't want to! Who will bring up my children? Who will take care of them? Who will love them? No, I don't want to!—I don't——"

She fell back. All was over.

The dog, wild with excitement, jumped around the room, barking.

Colombel ran to the window, calling his brother-in-law:

" Hurry up, hurry up! I think that she has just gone."

Then Cimme, resigned, arose and entered the room, mumbling:

" It didn't take as long as I thought it would! "

# Divorce

AITRE BONTRAN, a celebrated Parisian lawyer, who for the last ten years had been pleading and obtaining all the separations between ill-assorted couples, opened the door of his office and stepped aside to allow the new client to enter.

He was a large, red-faced, vigorous-looking man with blonde side whiskers. He bowed.

" Please be seated," said the lawyer.

The client sat down and cleared his throat:

" I come to retain your services, Monsieur, in a divorce case."

" I am listening."

" Monsieur, I am a former notary."

" So early! "

" Yes, so early. I am thirty-seven years old."

" Please continue."

"Monsieur, I have made an unfortunate marriage, a very unfortunate one."

"You are not the only one."

"I know it, and I pity the other ones; but my case is quite out of the ordinary and my grievances against my wife are rather peculiar. But I will begin at the beginning. I got married in a rather strange manner. Do you believe in peculiar ideas?"

"What do you mean by that?"

"Do you believe that certain ideas are as dangerous for some minds as poison is for the body?"

"Yes, perhaps."

"Certainly. There are ideas which get into our minds, which eat our hearts and kill us or make us go crazy if we do not know how to resist them. It is a sort of parasite living on our minds. If we are unfortunate enough to allow one of these ideas to slip into our minds, if we do not notice at the very beginning that it is an intruder and tyrant, that it extends itself, hour by hour, day by day, that it continually returns, drives away our other preoccupations, absorbs our attention and changes our point of view, if we do not observe these facts, then we are lost.

"Well, this is what happened to me, Monsieur. As I have already said, I was a notary at Rouen, not poor, but forced to observe a strict economy and to limit all my tastes! And that is hard at my age.

"As notary, I read with great care the advertisements on the last pages of the papers, the personals, etc., and in that manner I often arranged rather advantageous marriages for my clients.

"One day my attention was attracted to this:

"'Pretty, well-educated, respectable young lady

would marry an honorable man and bring him two
million five hundred thousand francs clear. Nothing
accepted from agencies.'

" I happened to be dining that day with two
friends, one a lawyer and the other a mill-owner.
Somehow or other, the conversation turned to marriages, and I told them, laughing, about the young
lady with the
two million five
hundred thou-
sand francs.

" The mill-
o w n e r said:
' What kind of
women are they,
as a rule?'

" The law-
yer, who had sev-
eral times seen
happy marriages
arise from these
conditions, gave
him details; then
he added, turn-
ing to me:

" ' W h y do
you not look into that yourself? Two and a half
million would relieve you of many of your cares.'

" The three of us laughed, and then we talked of
other things.

" An hour later I went home.

" It was cold that night. I lived in one of those
old-fashioned country houses. On putting my hand
on the iron bannister an icy shiver ran through me,
and as I stretched out the other hand to find the

wall I felt another damper chill course down my
back. The two seemed to meet in my chest and fill
my heart with sadness and pain. And, seized by a
sudden memory:

"'Jove! If I only had those two and a half
millions.'

"My room was gloomy; it was a bachelor's
room, taken care of by a servant who was also supposed to do the cooking. Can you imagine what that
room looked like? A large bed, no curtains, a closet,
a bureau, a wash-stand, and no fire. Clothes were
thrown on the chairs and papers littered the floor.
I began to hum a tune which I had heard in a concert
hall, for I sometimes go to those places:

"'Two million, two million looks good to me,
    With another half million any woman is fine.'

"I had not yet thought of the woman, and my
mind only turned to her as I slipp ' into bed, but
then I thought of her so much that I had difficulty
getting asleep.

"The following day, as I opened my eyes, before
daylight, I remembered that I had to be at Darmetal
before eight o'clock for some im ctant business.
Therefore I had to get up at six o' ock, and it was
freezing. By Jove! two million f ve hundr i 'hou-
sand!

"Toward ten o'clock I got back to my office.
There was the smell of a rusty sto e, of ol papers,
of shoes, of clothes, of everyth g, heate up to
eighty degrees.

"I lunched, as usual, on a rnt che i a piece
of cheese. Then I got to wor .

"It was then that I start l for th first time to
think seriously of the lady with the t million five

hundred thousand. Who was she? Why not write?
Why not find out?

" Well, Monsieur, to make a long story short, this
idea haunted me, tortured me for two weeks. All
my cares, all my little troubles, which I had always
borne without noticing them up to now, pricked me
like needles, and each one of these little griefs made
me think immediately of the lady with the two million five hundred thousand.

" I imagined her whole history. When one
wishes for something, Monsieur, one imagines it as
one would like to have it.

" Certainly, it was not natural for a young girl
of good family and with such a dowry to be looking
for a husband by advertisements. However, she
might be very honorable and unfortunate.

" First of all, this fortune of two million five
hundred thousand francs had not dazzled me as
something fairy-like. We notaries are accustomed
to reading all the offers of this nature and to seeing
proposals for marriage accompanied by six, eight,
ten, or even twelve millions. Twelve million is
rather common; it seems to please. I know that we
scarcely ever place any faith in the realization of
such promises. Nevertheless, they accustom our
mind to these fantastical figures, and make us consider a dowry of two million five hundred thousand
francs as very possible and very moral.

" Therefore a young girl, the natural child of a
*parvenu* and of a chambermaid, having suddenly inherited from her father, had learned at the same
time the shame of her birth, and, in order that she
might not have to disclose it to some man who might
have loved her, she was making use of this well-
known, much-used method of obtaining a life partner.

"My supposition was foolish. Nevertheless, I held on to it. We notaries ought never to read novels; and I have read many of them, Monsieur.

"Therefore I wrote to her as notary in the name of a client, and I waited.

"Five days later, at about three o'clock in the afternoon, I was working in my study when the head clerk came in and announced:

"'Mademoiselle Chantefrise.'

"'Show her in.'

"A woman of about thirty years of age, a little heavy, dark and with an embarrassed appearance, entered.

"'Please be seated, Mademoiselle.'

"She sat down and murmured:

"'It is I, Monsieur.'

"'But, Mademoiselle, I have not the honor of knowing you.'

"'I am the person to whom you wrote.'

"'About a marriage?'

"'Yes, Monsieur.'

"'Ah! very well.'

"'I came myself, because I think it is the best plan to conduct business personally.'

"'You are right, Mademoiselle. We say—you wish to get married?'

"'Yes, sir.'

"'Have you any family?'

"She hesitated, dropped her eyes and stammered:

"'No, sir. My father—and mother—are dead.'

"I started. I had guessed correctly, and a lively sympathy arose suddenly in my heart for this poor creature. I dropped the subject in order not to wound her, and I continued:

" ' Is your fortune clear? '

" She answered this time without hesitating:

" ' Oh! yes, sir.'

" I looked at her carefully, and really she did not displease me, although she was a little ripe, a little riper than I expected. She was a commanding, stately woman. The idea came to me to play a little comedy for her benefit, to fall in love with her and to supplant my imaginary client when I had ascertained that the dowry was not an illusion. I spoke to her of this client and depicted him as a sad, very honorable, but somewhat sickly man.

" She said quickly: ' Oh, Monsieur, I like healthy people.'

" ' You shall see him first, Mademoiselle, but not for three or four days, as he left yesterday for England.'

" ' Oh! what a bother,' she said.

" ' Yes and no. Are you in a hurry to return home? '

" ' Not at all.'

" ' Then stay here. I will try to amuse you.'

" ' That is very kind of you, Monsieur.'

" ' Are you stopping at a hotel? '

" ' She mentioned the best hotel in Rouen.

" ' Well, Mademoiselle, will you allow your future—lawyer to offer you a dinner this evening? '

" She hesitated, a little uneasy and undecided; then she made up her mind:

" ' Yes, Monsieur.'

" ' I shall come for you at seven o'clock.'

" ' Yes, Monsieur.'

" ' Good afternoon, Mademoiselle.'

" ' Good afternoon, Monsieur.'

" I saw her to the door.

"At seven o'clock I was at her place. She had dressed up for my sake and received me in a very charming manner.

"I took her to dinner in a restaurant where I was known, and the order that I gave was somewhat disquieting for my purse.

"An hour later we were great friends, and she was telling me the history of her life. The daughter of a great lady who had been wronged by a nobleman, she had been brought up on a farm. She was rich at present, having inherited large sums from both her father and her mother, whose names she would never, never tell. It would be useless to ask or to beg her to tell them, she never would. As I cared little about that, I questioned her about her fortune. She immediately started to talk in a practical manner, sure of her figures and titles, sure of her income, interests and investments. Her competence in this matter immediately gave me great confidence in her, and I became complimentary, although with reserve; but I showed her nevertheless that she pleased me.

"She became sentimental, although gracefully. I offered her some champagne and drank some myself, which made my ideas a little hazy. I then felt clearly that I was going to become bolder, and I was afraid, afraid of myself and of her, for fear that she, being also a little moved, might yield to me. In order to calm myself, I began once more to talk about the dowry, telling her that she would have to establish it exactly, as my client was a business man.

"She answered gaily: 'Oh! all right! I have brought all the proofs with me.'

"'Here, to Rouen?'

"'Yes, to Rouen.'

"'Have you them at the hotel?'

" ' Yes.'

" ' Can you show them to me? '

" ' Of course.'

" ' This evening? '

" ' Certainly.'

" This saved me in every way. I paid the bill, and we started for her place.

" She had indeed brought all the titles. There could no longer be any doubt; I was holding them, feeling them, reading them. This made me so happy that I was immediately seized by an overwhelming desire to kiss her. I did, once, twice, many times— so that, the champagne helping, I, or rather she, weakened—and yielded.

" Ah, Monsieur, you should have seen me afterward—and her! She was weeping like a fountain, begging me not to betray and abandon her. I promised anything that she wished, and I left her in a terrible state of mind.

" What was I to do? I had abused her confidence. That would have been nothing if I had had a client for her, but I had none. I was the simple, deceived client, betrayed by himself. What a predicament! True, I could drop her. But what about the dowry? And then, did I have the right to drop the poor girl after having surprised her? But what suspicions I should have later on!

" How little security I should have with a woman who yielded thus easily! I spent a restless night, tortured by remorse, fears and scruples. But in the morning my mind cleared. I dressed with care and presented myself at eleven o'clock at the hotel where she was staying.

" On seeing me, she blushed to the ears.

" I said to her:

"'Mademoiselle, I see only one way for me to repair our fault. I ask you for your hand.'

"She stammered:

"'I give it to you.'

"I married her.

"All went well for six months.

"I had given up my office and was living on my income, and really my wife was absolutely without reproach.

"Nevertheless, I noticed that from time to time she would stay out for several hours.

"This happened on regular days, one week on a Tuesday, another week on a Friday. I thought that she was deceiving me, and followed her.

"It was a Tuesday. She walked out at about one o'clock, walked down the Rue de la République, turned to the right through the street which follows the archepiscopal palace, took the Rue Grand-Pont down to the Seine, then she followed the quay to the Pierre bridge and crossed the river. From this moment on, she seemed uneasy, stopping often and watching all the passers-by.

"As I had disguised myself as a coal-heaver, she did not recognize me.

"Finally, she went into the railroad station. I no longer had any doubts, her lover would arrive by the one forty-five train.

"I hid behind a truck and waited. A whistle blew—a stream of passengers rushed out—she sprang forward, snatched up in her arms a little three-year-old girl who was accompanied by a peasant woman and kissed her passionately. Then she turned around, perceived another, younger child, carried by another peasant woman, and rushed toward it, snatching it in her arms and hugging it. She left, escorted by the two children and the two nurses, and went toward the long, somber and deserted walk of the Cours-la-Reine.

" I went home dazed, distressed in mind, understanding and not understanding, not daring to guess.

" When she returned for dinner I rushed toward her, shrieking:

" ' What are those children? '

" ' What children? '

" ' Those whom you were awaiting at the train from Saint Sever? '

" She screamed and fainted. When she came to she confessed to me in a flood of tears that she had four of them. Yes, sir, two for Tuesdays—two girls —and two boys for Fridays.

" And that was—oh, what shame—that was the origin of her fortune. The four fathers! . . . She had amassed her dowry.

" Now, Monsieur, what do you advise me to do? "

The lawyer answered solemnly:

" Recognize your children, Monsieur."

## Moiron

S we were still talking about Pranzini, M. Maloureau, who had been Attorney General under the Empire, said: " Oh! I formerly knew a very curious affair, curious for several reasons, as you will see.

" I was at that time Imperial Attorney in one of the provinces. I had to take up the case which has remained famous under the name of the Moiron case.

" Monsieur Moiron, who was a teacher in the North of France, enjoyed an excellent reputation throughout the whole country. He was a person of intelligence, quiet, very religious, a little taciturn; he had married in the District of Boislinot, where he exercised his profession. He had had three children, and each one of them had died from lung disease. From this time he seemed to bestow upon the youngsters confided to his care all the tenderness of his heart. With his own money he bought

toys for his best scholars and for the good boys; he
gave them little dinners and stuffed them with
delicacies, sweet things and cakes. Everybody loved
this good man with such a big heart, when suddenly, in a strange manner, five of his pupils died,
one after the other. People looked for an epidemic
in the water resulting from the drought; they looked
for the causes without being able to discover them,
the more so that the symptoms were so strange.
The children seemed to be attacked by a languishing sickness; they would no longer eat, they com-
plained of pains in their stomachs, dragged along
for a short time, and died in frightful suffering.

" A post-mortem examination was held over the
last one, but nothing was found. The vitals were
sent to Paris and analyzed, and they revealed the
presence of no toxic substance.

" For a year nothing new developed; then two
little boys, the best scholars in the class, Moiron's
favorites, died within four days of each other. An
examination of the bodies was again ordered, and
in both of them were discovered tiny fragments of
crushed glass. The conclusion arrived at was that
the two youngsters must imprudently have eaten
from some carelessly cleaned receptacle. A glass
broken over a pail of milk could have produced this
frightful accident, and the affair would have been
pushed no further if Moiron's servant had not been
taken sick at this time. The physician who was
called in noticed the same symptoms he had seen in
the children. He questioned her and obtained the
admission that she had stolen and eaten some con-
fections that had been bought by the teacher for his
scholars.

" On an order from the court the schoolhouse

was searched, and a closet was found which was full of toys and dainties destined for the children. Almost all these delicacies contained bits of crushed glass or pieces of broken needles!

" Moiron was immediately arrested; but he seemed so astonished and indignant at the suspicion hanging over him that he was almost released. However, indications of his guilt kept appearing, and I struggled in my mind with my first conviction, based on his excellent reputation, on his whole life, on the complete absence of any motives for such a crime.

" Why should this good, simple, religious man have killed children, and the very children whom he seemed to love the most, whom he spoiled and stuffed with sweet things, for whom he spent half his salary in buying toys and bonbons?

" One must believe him insane in order to think him guilty of this act. Now, Moiron seemed so normal, so quiet, so full of reason and common sense that it seemed impossible he should be touched by madness.

" However, the proofs kept growing! In none of the sweets that were bought at the places where the schoolmaster secured his provisions could the slightest fragment of anything suspicious be found.

" He then pretended that an unknown enemy must have opened his cupboard with a false key in order to introduce the glass and the needles into the eatables. And he imagined the whole story of an inheritance depending upon the death of a child, looked for by some peasant, and obtained thus, by casting suspicions on the schoolmaster. This brute, he claimed, did not care about the other children who were thus forced to die.

" The story was possible. The man appeared to be so sure of himself and in such despair that we should undoubtedly have acquitted him, notwithstanding the charges against him, if two crushing discoveries had not been made, one after the other.

" The first one was a snuffbox full of crushed glass; his own snuffbox, hidden in the desk where he kept his money!

" He explained this new find in an acceptable manner, as the ruse of the real unknown criminal. But a mercer from Saint-Marlof came to the presiding judge and said that a gentleman had several times come to his store to buy some needles; and he always asked for the thinnest needles he could find, and would break them to see whether they pleased him. The man was brought forward in the presence of a dozen or more persons, and immediately recognized Moiron. The inquest revealed that the schoolmaster had indeed gone into Saint-Marlof on the days mentioned by the tradesman.

" I will pass over the terrible testimony of children on the choice of dainties and the care which he took to have them eat the things before him, and to do away with the slightest trace.

" Public opinion became exasperated, and demanded capital punishment, and it became more and more insistent.

" Moiron was condemned to death, and his appeal was rejected. Nothing was left for him but the imperial pardon. I knew through my father that the Emperor would not grant it.

" One morning, as I was walking in my study, the visit of the prison almoner was announced. He was an old priest who knew men well and understood the habits of criminals. He seemed troubled,

ill at ease, nervous. After talking for a few minutes
about one thing and another, he arose and said suddenly: ' If Moiron is executed, Monsieur, you will
have killed an innocent man.'

" Then he left without bowing, leaving behind
him a deep impression with his words. He had pronounced them in such a sincere and solemn manner,
opening, in order to save a life, these lips closed
and sealed by the secret of confession.

" An hour later I left for Paris, and my father
immediately asked that I be granted an audience
with the Emperor.

" The following day I was received. His Maj-
esty was working in a little study when we were
introduced. I exposed the whole affair, and I was
just telling about the priest's visit when a door
opened behind the sovereign's chair and the Empress, who thought him alone, appeared. His Maj-
esty, Napoleon, consulted her. As soon as she had
heard the matter, she exclaimed: ' Since this man
is innocent, he must be pardoned.'

" Why did this sudden conviction of a religious
woman cast a terrible doubt in my mind?

" Until then I had ardently desired a change of
sentence. And now I suddenly felt myself the toy,
the dupe of a cunning criminal who had employed
the priest and confession as a last means of defense.

" I explained my hesitancy to their Majesties.
The Emperor remained undecided, urged on one
side by his natural kindness, and held back on the
other by the fear of being deceived by a criminal;
but the Empress, who was convinced that the priest
had obeyed a divine inspiration, kept repeating:
' Never mind! It is better to spare a criminal than
to kill an innocent man!' Her advice was taken.

The death sentence was commuted to one of hard labor.

"A few years later I heard that Moiron had again been called to the Emperor's attention on account of his exemplary conduct in the prison at Toulon, and was now employed as a servant by the director of the penitentiary.

"For a long time I heard nothing more of this man.

"But about two years ago, while I was spending a summer near Lille with my cousin, De Larielle, I was informed one evening, just as we were sitting down to dinner, that a young priest wished to speak to me.

"I had him shown in and he begged me to come to a dying man who desired absolutely to see me. This had often happened to me in my long career as a magistrate, and, although set aside by the Republic, I was still often called upon in similar circumstances. I, therefore, followed the priest, who led me to a miserable little room in a large tenement house.

"There I found a strange-looking man reclining on a bed of straw, with his back to the wall, in order better to breathe. He was a sort of skeleton, with dark, gleaming eyes.

"As soon as he saw me, he murmured: 'Don't you recognize me?'

"'No.'

"'I am Moiron.'

"I felt a shiver run through me, and I asked: 'The schoolmaster?'

"'Yes.'

"'How do you happen to be here?'

"'That story is too long, I haven't time to tell

it. . . . I was going to die . . . and that priest
was brought to me . . . and as I knew that you
were here I sent for you. . . . It is to you that
I wish to confess . . . since you were the one
who saved my life . . . formerly.'

" His hands contracted over the straw of his
bed; and he continued in a hoarse, energetic, and
low voice: ' You see . . . I owe you the truth
. . . I owe it to you . . . for it must be told
to some one before I leave this earth.

" ' It is I who killed the children . . . all of
them . . . I did it . . . for revenge!

" ' Listen. I was an honest, straightforward,
pure man . . . adoring God . . . this good
Father . . . this Master who teaches us to love,
and not the false God, the executioner, the robber,
the murderer who governs the earth. I had never
done any harm, I had never committed an evil act.
I was as good as it is possible to be, Monsieur.

" ' I married and had children, and I loved them
as no father or mother ever loved their children. I
lived only for them. I was wild about them. All
three of them died! Why? why? What had I done?
I felt revolted, furious; and suddenly my eyes were
opened as if I were waking up out of a sleep; I
understood that God is bad. Why had He killed my
children? I opened my eyes and saw that He loves
to kill. He loves only that, Monsieur. He gives
life but to destroy it! God, Monsieur, is a murderer! He needs death every day. And He makes
it in every variety, in order better to be amused.
He has invented sickness and accidents in order to
give Him diversion over the winter months and
through the years; and when He grows tired of
this, He has epidemics, the pest, cholera, diphtheria,

smallpox, everything possible! But this does not satisfy Him; all these things are too similar; and so from time to time He has wars, in order to see two hundred thousand soldiers killed at once, crushed in blood and in the mud, gutted, their arms and legs torn off, their heads smashed by bullets, like eggs falling on the pavement.

" ' But this is not all. He has made men who eat each other. And then, as men become better than He, He has made beasts, in order to see men hunt them, kill, and eat them. That is not all. He has made tiny little animals which live one day, flies who die by the millions in one hour, ants which we are continually crushing under our feet, and so many, many others that we cannot even imagine. And all these things are continually killing each other and dying. And the good Lord looks on and is amused, for He sees everything, the big ones as well as the little ones, those who are in the drops of water and those in the other firmaments. He watches them and is amused. Wretch!

" ' Then, Monsieur, I began to kill children. I played a trick on Him. He did not get those, it was I who did. Not he, but I! And I would have killed many others, but you caught me. There!

" ' I was to be executed. I! How He would have laughed! Then I asked for a priest, and I lied. I confessed. I lied and I lived.

" ' Now, all is over. I can no longer escape from Him. I no longer fear Him, Monsieur, I despise Him too much.'

" This poor wretch was frightful to see as he lay there gasping, opening an enormous mouth in order to let out words which could scarcely be heard, choking and spitting, picking at his bed and kicking around under a filthy sheet as though trying to escape.

"Oh! Even the memory of it is frightful!

"I asked him: 'You have nothing more to say?'

"'No, Monsieur.'

"'Then, farewell.'

"'Farewell, Monsieur, till some day . . .'

"I turned to the ashen-faced priest, whose dark outline stood out against the wall, and asked: 'Are you going to stay here, Monsieur l'Abbé?'

"'Yes.'

"Then the dying man cackled: 'Yes, yes, he sends the vultures to the corpses.'

"I had had enough of this; I opened the door and ran away."

## Madame Parisse

### I

WAS sitting on the pier of the small port of Obernon, near the village of Salis, looking at Antibes, bathed in the setting sun. I had never before seen anything so surprising and so beautiful.

The small town, inclosed by its heavy, protective walls, built by Monsieur de Vauban, reached out into the open sea, in the middle of the immense Gulf of Nice. The great waves, coming in from the ocean, broke at its feet, surrounding it with a wreath of foam; and beyond the ramparts the houses were climbing up the hill, one over the other, as far as the two towers which rose up into the sky, like the horns of an ancient helmet. And these two towers were outlined against the milky whiteness of the Alps, that enormous distant wall of snow which closed in the entire horizon.

Between the white foam at the foot of the walls and the white snow on the sky-line the little city, resting brilliant against the bluish background of the nearest mountain ranges, presented to the rays of the setting sun a pyramid of red-roofed houses, whose façades were also white, but so different one from another that they seemed of all tints.

And the sky above the Alps was itself of a blue that was almost white, as if the snow had tinted it; some silvery clouds were floating just over the pale summits, and on the other side of the Gulf of Nice, down by the water, unrolled like a white thread between the sea and the mountain. Two great sails, driven by a strong breeze, seemed to skim over the waves. I looked upon all this, astounded.

This view was one of those things so sweet, so rare, so delightful, that penetrate into you, and are unforgettable, like the memories of a joy. One sees, thinks, suffers, is moved, and loves with the eyes. He who can feel with the eye experiences the same keen, exquisite, and deep pleasure in looking upon men and things as the man with the delicate and sensitive ear, whose soul music overwhelms.

I turned to my companion, M. Martini, a pure-blooded Southerner.

" This is certainly one of the rarest sights which it has been vouchsafed to me to admire.

" I have seen the Mont Saint-Michel, this monstrous granite jewel, rise out of the sand at sunrise.

" I have seen, in the Sahara, Lake Raianechergui, fifty kilometers long, shining under a moon as brilliant as our sun and breathing up to it a white cloud, like a mist of milk.

" I have seen, in the Liparian Islands, the fan-

tastic sulphur crater of the Volcanello, a giant
flower which fumes and burns, an over-big yellow
flower, opening full on the sea, whose stem is a
volcano.

" But I have seen nothing more surprising than
Antibes, standing against the Alps at the setting sun.

" And I know not how it is that memories of
antiquity haunt me; verses of Homer come into my
mind; this is a city of the ancient East, a city out
of the Odyssey; this is Troy, although Troy was
very far from the sea."

M. Martini drew the Sarty guide-book out of
his pocket and read: " This city was originally a
colony founded by the Phocians of Marseilles,
about 340 B. C. They gave it the Greek name of
Antipolis, meaning counter-city, city opposite another, because it is in fact opposite to Nice, another colony from Marseilles.

" After the Gauls were conquered, the Romans
turned Antibes into a municipal city, its inhabitants
receiving the rights of Roman citizenship.

" We know by an epigram of Martial that at his
time——"

I interrupted him:

" I don't care what she was. I tell you that I
see down there a city out of the Odyssey. The coast
of Asia and the coast of Europe resemble each other
in their shores, and there is no city on the other
coast of the Mediterranean which awakens in me
the memories of the heroic times as this one does."

A footstep caused me to turn my head; a woman,
a large, dark woman, was walking along the road
which skirts the sea in going to the cape.

" That is Madame Parisse, you know," muttered
Monsieur Martini, dwelling on the final syllable.

No, I did not know, but that name, pronounced nonchalantly, that name of the Trojan shepherd, confirmed me in my dream.

Yet I asked: " Who is this Madame Parisse? "

He seemed astonished that I did not know the story.

· I assured him that I did not know it, and I looked after the woman, who passed by without seeing us, dreaming, walking with steady and slow step, as doubtless the ladies of old walked.

She was perhaps thirty-five years old, and still very beautiful, though a trifle stout.

And Monsieur Martini told me the following story:

## II

Mademoiselle Combelombe was married, one year before the war of 1870, to Monsieur Parisse, a government official. She was then a handsome young girl, as slender and lively as she has now become stout and sad.

Unwillingly she had accepted Monsieur Parisse, one of those little fat men with short legs, who trip along, with trousers always too large.

After the war Antibes was occupied by a single battalion commanded by Monsieur Jean de Carmelin, a young officer decorated during the war, and who had just received his four stripes.

As he found life exceedingly tedious in this fortress, this stuffy mole-hole inclosed by the enormous double walls, he often strolled out to the cape, a kind of park or pine wood whipped by all the winds from the sea.

There he met Madame Parisse, who also came out in the summer evenings to get the fresh air under the trees. How did they love each other? Who knows? They met, they looked at each other, and when out of sight they doubtless thought of each other. The image of the young woman with the brown eyes, the black hair, the pale skin, this fresh, handsome Southerner, who displayed her teeth in smiling, was floating before the eyes of the officer as he continued with his promenade, biting his cigar instead of smoking; and the image of the commanding officer, in his close-fitting coat, covered with gold, and his red trousers, with a little blond mustache, would pass in the evening before the eyes of Madame Parisse, when her husband, half shaven and ill-clad, short-legged and big-bellied, came home to supper.

Meeting so often, they perhaps smiled at the next meeting; then, seeing each other again and again, they thought that they knew each other. He certainly bowed to her. And she, surprised, bowed in return, but very, very slightly, just enough not to appear impolite. But after two weeks she returned his salutation away off, even before they were side by side.

He spoke to her. Of what? Doubtless of the setting sun. They admired it together, looking for it in each other's eyes more often than on the horizon. And every evening for two weeks this was the commonplace and persistent pretext for a few minutes' chat.

Then they hazarded a few steps together, talking of anything that came along, but their eyes were already saying to each other a thousand more intimate things, those secret, charming things that

are reflected in the gentle emotion of the eye, and
that cause the heart to beat, for they are a better
confession of the soul than the spoken word.

And then he would take her hand, murmuring
those words which the woman divines, without seem-
ing to hear them.

And it was agreed between them that they would
love each other without making proof of it by anything sensual or brutal.

She would have remained indefinitely at this
stage of intimacy, but he wanted more. And every
day he urged her more hotly to give in to his violent
desire.

She resisted, she did not want it, she seemed
determined not to give way.

Yet one evening she said to him, casually: " My
husband has just gone to Marseilles. He will be
away four days."

Jean de Carmelin threw himself at her feet,
imploring her to open her door to him that very
night at eleven o'clock. But she would not listen
to him, and went home with angry mien.

The commander was in bad humor all the evening, and the next morning at dawn he went out
on the ramparts in a rage, from one exercise
field to the other, dealing out punishments to the
officers and men as one might fling stones into a
crowd.

On coming back for his breakfast, he found an
envelope under his napkin with these four words:
" To-night at ten." And he gave one hundred sous
off-hand to the waiter serving him.

The day seemed endless to him. He passed part
of it in curling his hair and perfuming himself.

As he was sitting down to the dinner-table, another envelope was handed to him, and in it he found the following telegram:

"My Love: Business done. I return this evening on the nine o'clock train. Parisse."

The commander let loose such a big oath that the waiter dropped the soup-tureen on the floor.

What should he do? He certainly wanted her, that very evening, at whatever cost; and he would have her. He would resort to any means, even to arresting and imprisoning the husband. Then a mad thought struck him. Calling for paper, he wrote the following note:

"Madame: He will not come back this evening, I swear it to you, and I shall be where you know at ten o'clock. Fear nothing. I will answer for everything, on my honor as officer. Jean de Carmelin."

And having sent off this letter, he calmly dined.

Toward eight o'clock he sent for Captain Gribois, the second in command, and he said, rolling between his fingers the crumpled telegram of Monsieur Parisse:

" Captain, I have just received a telegram of a very singular nature, which it is impossible for me to communicate to you. You will immediately have all the gates of the city closed and guarded, so that no one, mind me, no one, will either enter or leave before six in the morning. You will also have men patrol the streets, who will compel the inhabitants to retire to their houses at nine o'clock. And one found outside beyond that time will be conducted to his home *manu militari*. If your men meet me this night they will at once go out of my way, appearing not to know me. You understand me? "

" Yes, Commander."

" I hold you responsible for the execution of my orders, my dear Captain."

" Yes, Commander."

" Would you like to have a glass of char-treuse? "

" With great pleasure, Commander."

They clinked glasses, drank down the brown liquor, and Captain Gribois left the room.


## III


The train from Marseilles arrived at the station at nine o'clock sharp, left two passengers on the platform, and went on toward Nice.

One of them, tall and thin, was Monsieur Saribe, the oil merchant, and the other, short and fat, was Monsieur Parisse.

Together they set out, with their valises, to reach the city, one kilometer distant.

But on arriving at the gate of the port the guards crossed their bayonets, commanding them to retire.

Frightened, surprised, cowed with astonishment, they retired to deliberate; then, after having taken counsel one with the other, they came back cautiously to parley, giving their names.

But the soldiers evidently had strict orders, for they threatened to shoot; and the two scared travelers ran off, throwing away their valises, which impeded their flight.

Making the tour of the ramparts, they presented themselves at the gate on the route to Cannes. This likewise was closed and guarded by a menacing sentinel. Messrs. Saribe and Parisse, like the prudent men they were, desisted from their efforts, and went back to the station for shelter, since it was not safe to be near the fortification after sundown.

The station agent, surprised and somnolent, permitted them to stay till morning in the waiting-room.

And they sat there side by side, in the dark, on the green velvet sofa, too scared to think of sleeping.

It was a long and weary night for them.

At half-past six in the morning they were informed that the gates were open, and that people could now enter Antibes.

They set out for the city, but they failed to find their abandoned valises on the road.

When they passed through the gates of the city, still somewhat anxious, the Commandant de Carmelin, with sly glance and mustache turned up, came himself to look over and examine them.

Then he bowed to them politely, excusing himself for having caused them a bad night. But he had to carry out orders.

The people of Antibes were scared to death. Some spoke of a surprise planned by the Italians; others, of the landing of the Prince Imperial; and others, again, believed that there was an Orléanist conspiracy. The truth was suspected only later, when it became known that the battalion of the Commandant had been sent very far away, and that Monsieur de Carmelin had been severely punished.

## IV

Monsieur Martini had finished his story. Madame Parisse returned, her promenade being terminated. She passed gravely near me, with her eyes fixed on the Alps, whose summits now gleamed rosy in the last rays of the setting sun.

I felt like saluting her, this poor, sad woman, who would ever be thinking of that night of love, now far distant, and of the bold man who for the sake of a kiss from her had dared to put a city into a state of siege and to compromise his whole future.

And to-day he had probably forgotten her, if he did not relate this audacious, comical, and tender farce to his comrades over the cups.

Had she seen him again? Did she still love him? And I thought: Here is an instance of modern love, grotesque and yet heroic. The Homer to sing of this new Helena and the adventure of her Menelaus must be gifted with the soul of Paul de Kock. And yet the hero of this deserted woman was brave, daring, handsome, strong, like Achilles, and more cunning than Ulysses.

# The Penguins' Rock

HIS is the season for penguins.

From April to the end of May, before the Parisian visitors arrive, one sees, all at once, on the little beach at Etretat, several old men, booted and belted in shooting costume. They spend four or five days at the Hôtel Hanville, disappear, and return again three weeks later. Then, after a fresh sojourn, they go away altogether.

One sees them again the following spring.

These are the last gull hunters, what remain of the old set. There were about twenty enthusiasts thirty or forty years ago; now there are only a few of those enthusiastic sportsmen.

The penguin is a very rare bird of passage, with peculiar habits. It lives the greater part of the year in the latitude of Newfoundland and the islands of St. Pierre and Miquelon. But in the breeding season a flock of emigrants cross the ocean and come every year to the same spot to lay their eggs, to the Penguins' Rock, near Etretat. They are found nowhere else, only there. They have always come there, have always been chased away, but return again, and will always return. As soon as the young birds are grown they all fly away and disappear for a year.

Why do they not go elsewhere? Why not choose some other spot on the long, white, unending cliff that extends from the Pas-de-Calais to Havre? What force, what invincible instinct, what custom of centuries impels these birds to come back to this place? What first migration, what tempest, possi bly, once cast their ancestors on this rock? And why do the children, the grandchildren, all the descendants of the first parents, always return here?

There are not many of them, a hundred at most, as if one single family, maintaining the tradition, made this annual pilgrimage.

And each spring, as soon as the little wandering tribe has taken up its abode on the rock, the same sportsmen also reappear in the village. One knew them formerly when they were young; now they are old, but constant to the regular appointment which they have kept for thirty or forty years. They would not miss it for anything in the world.


It was an April evening in one of the later years. Three of the old sportsmen had arrived; one was missing—Monsieur d'Arnelles.

He had written to no one, given no account of

himself. But he was not dead, like so many of the rest; they would have heard of it. At length, tired of waiting for him, the other three sat down to table. Dinner was almost over, when a carriage drove into the yard of the hotel, and the late comer presently entered the dining-room.

He sat down, in a good humor, rubbing his hands, and ate with zest. When one of his comrades remarked, with surprise, at his being in a frock-coat, he replied quietly:

" Yes, I had no time to change my clothes."

They retired, on leaving the table, for they had to set out before daybreak in order to take the birds unawares.

There is nothing so pretty as this sport, this early morning expedition.

At three o'clock in the morning the sailors awoke the sportsmen by throwing sand against the windows. They were ready in a few minutes, and went down to the beach. Although it was still dark, the stars had paled a little. The sea ground the shingles on the beach. There was such a fresh breeze that it made one shiver slightly in spite of one's heavy clothing.

Presently two boats were pushed down the beach by the sailors with a sound as of tearing cloth, and were floated on the nearest waves. The brown sail was hoisted, swelled a little, fluttered, hesitated, swelled out again as round as a paunch, and carried the boats toward the large, arched entrance that could be faintly distinguished in the darkness.

The sky became clearer, the shadows seemed to melt away. The coast still seemed veiled, the great white coast, perpendicular as a wall.

They passed through the Manne-Porte, an enor-

mous arch beneath which a ship could sail; they
doubled the promontory of La Courtine, passed the
little valley of Antifer and the cape of the same
name, and suddenly caught sight of a beach on
which some hundreds of seagulls were perched.

That was the Seagulls' Rock. It was just a little protuberance of the cliff, and on the narrow
ledges of rock the birds' heads might be seen watching the boats.

They remained there, motionless, not venturing
to fly off as yet. Some of them perched on the
edges seated upright looked almost like bottles, for
their little legs are so short that when they walk
they glide along as if they were on rollers. When
they start to fly they cannot make a spring, and let
themselves fall like stones almost down to the very
men who are watching them.

They know their limitation and the danger to
which it subjects them, and cannot make up their
minds to fly away.

But the boatmen begin to shout, beating the sides
of the boat with the wooden boat pins, and the birds,
in affright, fly, one by one, into space until they
reach the level of the waves. Then, moving their
wings rapidly, they scud, scud along until they reach
the open sea, if a shower of lead does not knock
them into the water.

For an hour the firing is kept up, obliging them
to give up, one after another. Sometimes the mother birds will not leave their nests, and are riddled
with shot, causing drops of blood to spurt out on
the white cliff, and the animal dies without having
deserted her eggs.

The first day Monsieur d'Arnelles fired at the
birds with his habitual zeal; but when the party re-

turned, toward ten o'clock, beneath a brilliant sun, which cast great triangles of light on the white cliffs along the coast, he appeared worried and ab-sent-minded, contrary to his accustomed manner.

As soon as they got on shore a kind of servant dressed in black came up to him and said something in a low tone. He seemed to reflect, hesitate, and then replied:

" No; to-morrow."

The following day they set out again. This time Monsieur d'Arnelles frequently missed his aim, although the birds were close by. His friends teased him, asked him if he were in love, if some secret sorrow was troubling his mind and heart. At length he confessed:

" Yes, indeed. I have to leave soon, and that annoys me."

" What! you must leave? And why? "

" Oh, I have some business that calls me back. I cannot stay any longer."

They then talked of other matters.

As soon as breakfast was over the valet in black reappeared. Monsieur d'Arnelles ordered his carriage, and the man was leaving the room when the three sportsmen interfered, insisting, begging, and praying their friend to stay. One of them at last said:

" Come, now, this cannot be a matter of such importance, for you have already waited two days."

Monsieur d'Arnelles, altogether perplexed, began to think, evidently baffled, divided between pleasure and duty, unhappy and disturbed.

After reflecting for some time he stammered:

" The fact is—the fact is—I am not alone here. I have my son-in-law."

There were exclamations and shouts of:

"Your son-in-law! Where is he?"

He suddenly appeared confused, and his face grew red.

"What! Do you not know? Why—why—he is in the coach house. He is dead."

They were all silent, in amazement.

Monsieur d'Arnelles continued, more and more disturbed:

"I had the misfortune to lose him, and as I was taking the body to my house, in Briseville, I came round this way so as not to miss our appointment. But you can see that I cannot wait any longer."

Then one of the sportsmen, bolder than the rest, said:

"Well, but—since he is dead—it seems to me—that he can wait a day longer."

The others chimed in:

"That cannot be denied."

Monsieur d'Arnelles appeared to be relieved of a great weight; but a little uneasy, nevertheless, he asked:

"But frankly—do you think——"

The three others, as one man, replied:

"*Parbleu!* my dear boy, two days more or less can make no difference, in his present condition."

And, perfectly calmly, the father-in-law turned to the undertaker's assistant and said:

"Well, then, my friend, it will be the day after to-morrow."

# The Legend of Mont Saint-Michel

 HAD first seen this fairy-like castle in the sea from Cancale. It had looked to me like a confused mass, like a gray shadow rising in the foggy sky. I saw it again from Avranche at sunset. The immense stretch of sand was red, the horizon was red, the whole boundless bay was red; alone, the castle, growing out there in the distance like a fantastic manor, like a dream palace, strange and beautiful—this alone remained almost black in the brilliancy of the dying day.

The following morning at dawn I went toward it across the sands. My eyes fastened on this gigantic jewel, as big as a mountain, cut like a cameo, and as dainty as lace. The nearer I approached the greater my admiration grew, for nothing in the world could be more wonderful or more perfect.

As surprised as if I had discovered the habitation of a god, I wandered through those halls supported by frail or massive columns, raising my eyes in wonder to those spires which looked like rockets starting for the sky, and to that incredible crowd of towers, of gargoyles, of slender and charming ornaments, a regular fireworks of stone, granite lace, a masterpiece of colossal and delicate architecture.

As I was looking up in ecstasy, a Lower Normandy peasant came up to me and told me the story of the great quarrel between Saint Michel and the Devil.

A skeptical genius has said: "God made man as his image; man has returned the compliment."

This saying is an eternal truth, and it would be very curious to write the history of the local divinity on every continent, as well as the history of the patron saints in each one of the provinces. The negro has his ferocious man-eating idols; the polygamous Mahometan fills his paradise with women; the Greeks, like a practical people, have deified all the passions.

Every village in France is under the influence of some protecting saint, modeled according to the characteristics of the inhabitants.

Saint Michel watches over Lower Normandy, Saint Michel, the radiant and victorious angel, the sword-carrier, the hero of Heaven, the victorious, the conqueror of Satan.

But this is how the Lower Normandy peasant, cunning, underhanded, and tricky, understands and tells of the struggle between the great Saint and the Devil.

To escape from the malice of his neighbor the Demon, Saint Michel built himself, in the open ocean, this habitation worthy of an archangel; and only such a saint could build a residence of such magnificence.

But, as he still feared the approaches of the Wicked One, he surrounded his domains by quicksands, more treacherous even than water.

The Devil lived in a humble cottage on the hill; but he owned all the salt marshes, the rich lands where grow the finest crops, the wooded valleys, and all the fertile hills of the country; but the Saint ruled only over the sands. Therefore Satan was rich, whereas Saint Michel was as poor as a church mouse.

After a few years of fasting the Saint grew tired of this state of affairs, and began to think of some compromise with the Devil; but the matter was by no means easy, as Satan kept a good hold on his crops.

He thought the thing over for about six months; then one morning he set out for land. The Demon was eating his soup in front of his door when he saw the Saint; he immediately rushed toward him, kissed the hem of his sleeve, invited him in, and offered him refreshments.

Saint Michel drank a bowl of milk and then began: " I have come here to propose to you a good bargain."

The Devil, candid and trustful, answered: " Very well."

" Here it is. Give me all your lands."

Satan, growing alarmed, wished to speak: " But——"

The Saint continued: " Listen first. Give me all your lands. I will take care of all the work, the plowing, the sowing, the fertilizing, everything, and we will share the crops equally. How does that suit you? "

The Devil, who was naturally lazy, accepted. He

only asked in addition for a few of those delicious *surmullets* which can be caught around the solitary mountain. Saint Michel promised the fish.

They shook hands and spat to show that it was a bargain, and the Saint continued: "Here, so that you will have nothing to complain of, choose that part of the crops which you prefer: that which will be above ground, or in the ground. Satan cried out: "I choose all that will be above ground."

"It's a bargain!" said the Saint. And he went away.

Six months later, all over the immense domain of the Devil, one could see nothing but carrots, turnips, onions, salsify, all the plants whose juicy roots are good and savory, and whose useless leaves are good for nothing but for feeding animals.

Satan wished to break the contract, calling Saint Michel a swindler.

But the Saint, who had developed quite a taste for agriculture, went back to see the Devil, and said: "Really, I hadn't thought of that at all; it was just an accident, no fault of mine. And to make things fair with you, this year I'll let you take everything that is under the ground."

"Very well," answered Satan.

The following spring, all the Evil Spirit's lands were covered with golden wheat, oats as big as beans, linseed, magnificent colzas, red clover, peas, cabbage, artichokes, everything that blossoms into grains or fruit in the sunlight.

Once more Satan received nothing, and this time he completely lost his temper. He took back his fields and remained deaf to all the new propositions of his neighbor.

A whole year rolled by. From the top of his

lonely manor, Saint Michel looked at the distant
and fertile lands, and watched the Devil direct the
work, take in his crops, and thresh the wheat. And
he grew angry, exasperated at his powerlessness.
As he was no longer able to deceive Satan, he decided to reap vengeance on him, and he went out to
invite him to dinner for the following Monday.

"You have been very unfortunate in your deal-
ings with me," he said; "I know it; but I don't
want any ill feeling between us, and I expect you to
dine with me. I'll give you some good things to
eat."

Satan, who was as greedy as he was lazy, accepted eagerly. On the day which had been decided
on, he donned his finest clothes and set out for the
castle.

Saint Michel sat him down to a magnificent meal.
First there was a *vol-au-vent,* full of cocks' crests
and kidneys, with meat-balls, then two big *surmullets* with cream sauce, a turkey stuffed with chest-
nuts soaked in wine, some salt-marsh lamb as tender
as possible, vegetables which melted in the mouth,
and nice warm cake which was brought on smoking
and spreading a delicious odor of butter.

They drank hard and sparkling cider, and red
wine both flat and sparkling, and after each course
more room was made with some old apple brandy.

The Devil drank and ate to his heart's content;
in fact, he took so much that he found himself in-
convenienced.

Then Saint Michel arose in anger, and cried, in
a voice like thunder: "What! before me, rascal!
you dare—before me——"

Satan, terrified, ran away, and the Saint, seizing a stick, pursued him. They ran around through

the halls, turning around the pillars, running up the staircases, galloping along the cornices, jumping from gargoyle to gargoyle. The poor Demon, who was woefully ill, was running about madly and soiling the Saint's home. At last he found himself at the top of the last terrace, from which could be seen the immense bay, with its distant cities, sands, and passages. He could no longer escape, and the Saint came up behind him and gave him a furious kick, which shot him through space like a cannon-ball.

He shot through the air like a javelin and fell heavily before the town of Mortain. His horns and claws stuck deep into the rock, which keeps through eternity the traces of this fall of Satan's.

He stood up again, limping, crippled until the end of time, and as he looked at this fatal castle in the distance, standing out against the setting sun, he understood well that he would always be vanquished in this unequal struggle; and he went away limping, heading for distant countries, leaving to his enemy his fields, his hills, his valleys, and his marshes.

And this is how Saint Michel, the patron saint of Normandy, vanquished the Devil.

Another people would have dreamed of this battle in an entirely different manner.

# Martine

T came to him one Sunday after mass. He was walking home from church, along the hollow road that led to his house, when he saw ahead of him Martine, who was also going home.

Her father walked beside his daughter with the important gait of a wealthy farmer. Discarding the smock, he wore a short coat of gray cloth and on his head a round-topped hat with wide brim.

She, laced up in a corset which she wore only once a week, walked along erect, with her squeezed-in waist, her broad shoulders, and prominent hips, swinging herself a little. She wore a hat trimmed with flowers, made by a milliner at Yvetot, and displayed the back of her full, round, supple neck, reddened by the sun and air, on which fluttered little stray locks of hair.

Benoist saw only her back; but he knew well the face he loved, without, however, having ever noticed it more closely than he did now.

Suddenly he said: "*Nom d'un nom,* she is a fine girl, all the same, that Martine." He watched her as she walked, admiring her hastily, feeling a desire taking possession of him. He did not long to see her face again, no. He kept gazing at her figure, repeating to himself: "*Nom d'un nom,* she is a fine girl."

Martine turned to the right, to enter "La Martinière," the farm of her father, Jean Martin; and she cast a glance behind her as she turned round. She saw Benoist, who looked to her very comical. She called out: "Good morning, Benoist." He replied: "Good morning, Martine; good morning, Maît' Martin," and went on his way.

When he reached home the soup was on the table. He sat down opposite his mother beside the farm-hand and the hired man, while the maid-servant went to draw some cider.

He ate a few spoonsful, then pushed away his plate. His mother said:

"Don't you feel well?"

"No, I feel as if I had some pap in my stomach, and that takes away my appetite."

He watched the others eating as he cut himself a piece of bread from time to time and carried it lazily to his mouth, masticating it slowly. He thought of Martine. "She is a fine girl, all the same." And to think that he had not noticed it before, and that it came to him, just like that, all at once, and with such force that he could hardly eat.

He did not touch the stew. His mother said:

"Come, Benoist, try and eat a little; it is loin of mutton; it will do you good. When one has no appetite, he should force himself to eat."

He swallowed a few morsels, then, pushing away
his plate, said:

"No. I can't go that, positively."

When they rose from table he walked round the
farm, telling the farm-hand he might go home, and
that he would drive up the animals as he passed
them.

The country was deserted as it was the day of
rest. Here and there, in a field of clover, cows were
moving along heavily, with full bellies, chewing
their cud under a blazing sun. Unharnessed plows
were standing at the end of a furrow, and the up-
turned earth ready for the seed showed broad,
brown patches amid yellow patches of stubble
of wheat and oats that had lately been har-
vested.

A rather dry autumn wind blew across the plain,
promising a cool evening after the sun had set.
Benoist sat down on a ditch, placed his hat on his
knees as if he needed to cool off his head, and said
aloud in the stillness of the country: "If you want
a fine girl, she is a fine girl."

He thought of it again at night, in his bed, and
in the morning when he awoke.

He was not sad, he was not discontented, he
could not have told what ailed him. It was something that had hold of him, something fastened
in his mind, an idea that would not leave him
and that produced a sort of tickling sensation in
his heart.

Sometimes a big fly is shut up in a room. You
hear it flying about, buzzing, and the noise haunts
you, irritates you. Suddenly it stops; you forget it; but all at once it begins again, obliging you
to look up. You cannot catch it, nor drive it away,

nor kill it, nor make it keep still. As soon as it settles for a second it instantly starts off buzzing again.

The recollection of Martine disturbed Benoist's mind like an imprisoned fly.

Then he longed to see her again, and walked past the Martinière several times. He saw her, at last, hanging out some clothes on a line stretched between two apple trees.

It was a warm day. She had on only a short skirt and her chemise, showing the curves of her figure as she hung up the towels. He remained there concealed by the hedge for more than an hour, even after she had left. He returned home more obsessed with her image than ever.

For a month his mind was full of her, he trembled when her name was mentioned in his presence. He could not eat, he had night sweats that kept him from sleeping.

On Sunday, at mass, he never took his eyes off her. She noticed it, and smiled at him, flattered at his appreciation.

One evening he suddenly met her in the road. She stopped short when she saw him coming. Then he walked right up to her, choking with fear and emotion, but determined to speak to her. He began falteringly:

"See here, Martine, this cannot go on like this any longer."

She replied, as if she wanted to tease him:

"What cannot go on any longer, Benoist?"

"My thinking of you as many hours as there are in the day," he answered.

She put her hands on her hips.

"I do not oblige you to do so."

"Yes, it is you," he stammered; "I cannot sleep, nor rest, nor eat, nor anything."

"What do you need to cure you of all that?" she asked.

He stood there in dismay, his arms swinging, his eyes staring, his mouth agape.

She hit him a punch in the stomach, and ran off.

From that day they met each other along the roadside, in byroads, or' else at twilight on the edge of a field, when he was going home with his horses and she was driving her cows home to the stable.

He felt himself carried, cast toward her by a strong impulse of his heart and body. He would have liked to squeeze her, strangle her, eat her, make her part of himself. And he trembled with impotence, impatience, rage, to think she did not belong to him entirely, as if they were one being.

People gossiped about it in the countryside. They said they were engaged. He had, however, asked her if she would be his wife, and she had answered: "Yes."

They were waiting for an opportunity to talk to their parents about it.

But all at once she stopped coming to meet him at the usual hour. He did not even see her as he wandered round the farm. He could only catch a glimpse of her at mass on Sunday. And one Sunday, after the sermon, the priest actually published the banns of marriage between Victoire-Adelaide Martin and Josephin-Isidore Vallin.

Benoist felt a sensation in his hands as if the blood had been drained off. He had a buzzing in the ears, and could hear nothing; and presently he perceived that his tears were falling on his prayer book.

For a month he stayed in his room. Then he went back to his work.

But he was not cured, and it was always in his mind. He avoided the roads that led past her home, so that he might not even see the trees in the yard, and this obliged him to make a great circuit morning and evening.

She was now married to Vallin, the richest farmer in the district. Benoist and he did not speak now, though they had been comrades from childhood.

One evening, as Benoist was passing the town hall, he heard that she was *enceinte*. Instead of experiencing a feeling of sorrow, he experienced, on the contrary, a feeling of relief. It was over now, all over. They were more separated by that than by her marriage. He really preferred that it should be so.

Months passed, and more months. He caught sight of her occasionally going to the village with a heavier step than usual. She blushed as she saw him, lowered her head, and quickened her pace. And he turned out of his way so as not to pass her and meet her glance.

He dreaded the thought that he might one morning meet her face to face and be obliged to speak to her. What could he say to her now after all he had said formerly when he held her hands as he kissed her hair beside her cheeks? He often thought of those meetings along the roadside. She had acted falsely after all her promises.

By degrees his grief diminished, leaving only sadness behind. And one day he took the old road that led past the farm where she now lived. He looked at the roof from a distance. It was there, in there, that she lived, with another! The apple

trees were in bloom, the cocks crowed on the dung-
hill. The whole dwelling seemed empty, the farm-
hands had gone to the fields to their spring toil.
He stopped near the gate and looked into the yard.
The dog was asleep outside his kennel. Three calves
were walking slowly, one behind the other, toward
the pond. A big turkey was strutting before the
door, parading before the turkey hens like a singer
at the opera.

Benoist leaned against the gatepost and was
suddenly seized with a desire to weep. But suddenly he heard a cry, a loud cry for help, coming
from the house. He was struck with dismay, his
hands grasping the wooden bars of the gate, and
listened attentively. Another cry, a prolonged,
heartrending cry, reached his ears, his soul, his
flesh. It was she who was crying like that! He
darted inside, crossed the grass patch, pushed open
the door, and saw her lying on the floor, her body
drawn up, her face livid, her eyes haggard, in the
throes of childbirth.

He stood there, trembling and paler than she
was, and stammered:

" Here I am, here I am, Martine! "

She replied in gasps:

" Oh, do not leave me, do not leave me, Benoist! "

He looked at her, not knowing what to say, what
to do. She began to cry out again:

" Oh! oh! it is killing me. Oh, Benoist! "

She writhed frightfully.

Benoist was suddenly seized with a frantic longing to help her, to quiet her, to remove her pain. He
leaned over, lifted her up, and laid her on her
bed; and while she kept on moaning he began to

take off her clothes, her jacket, her skirt, and her petticoat. She bit her fists to keep from crying out. Then he did as he was accustomed to doing for cows, ewes, and mares; he assisted in delivering her, and found in his hands a large infant, who was moaning.

He wiped it off and wrapped it up in a towel that was drying in front of the fire, and laid it on a bundle of clothes ready for ironing that was on the table. Then he went back to the mother.

He took her up and placed her on the floor again, then he changed the bedclothes and put her back into bed. She faltered:

"Thank you, Benoist; you have a noble heart." And then she wept a little, as if she felt regretful.

He did not love her any more, not the least bit. It was all over. Why? How? He could not have said. What had happened had cured him better than ten years of absence.

She asked, exhausted and trembling:

"What is it?"

He replied calmly:

"It is a very fine girl."

Then they were silent again. At the end of a few seconds the mother, in a weak voice, said:

"Show her to me, Benoist."

He took up the little one and was showing it to her as if he were holding the consecrated wafer, when the door opened and Isidore Vallin appeared.

He did not understand at first; then, all at once, he guessed.

Benoist, in consternation, stammered out:

"I was passing, I was just passing by when I heard her crying out, and I came—there is your child, Vallin!"

Then the husband, his eyes full of tears, stepped forward, took the little mite of humanity that he held out to him, kissed it, unable to speak from emotion for a few seconds; then, placing the child on the bed, he held out both hands to Benoist, saying:

" Your hand upon it, Benoist. From now on we understand each other. If you are willing, we will be a pair of friends, a pair of friends! "

And Benoist replied:

" Indeed I will; certainly; indeed, I will."

## The Fathers

HAVE a friend, Jean de Valnoix, whom I visit from time to time. He lives in a little cottage in the woods at the edge of a river. He retired from Paris after leading a wild life for fifteen years. Suddenly he had enough of pleasures, dinners, men, women, cards, everything; and he came to live in this little place where he had been born.

There are two or three of us who go, from time to time, to spend a few weeks with him. He is certainly delighted to see us when we arrive, and pleased to be alone again when we finally take our leave.

I went to see him last week, and he received me with open arms. We would spend hours at a time, sometimes together, sometimes alone. Usually he reads and I work during the daytime, and every evening we talk until midnight.

Well, last Tuesday, after a scorching day, toward

nine o'clock in the evening we were both of us sitting and watching the water flow at our feet; we were exchanging very vague ideas about the stars which were bathing in the current and which seemed to swim along ahead of us. Our ideas were very vague, confused, and brief, for our minds are very limited, weak, and powerless. I was expatiating on the sun that dies in the Great Bear. One can only see it on very clear nights, it is so pale. When the sky is the least bit clouded it disappears. We were thinking of the creatures which people these worlds, of their possible forms, of their unthinkable faculties and unknown organs, of the animals and plants of every kind, of all the things which man's dreams can barely touch.

Suddenly a voice called from the distance: "Monsieur, Monsieur!"

Jean answered: "Here I am, Baptiste!"

When the servant had found us he announced: "It's Monsieur's gypsy."

My friend burst out laughing, a thing which he rarely did, then he asked: "Is to-day the nineteenth of July?"

"Yes, Monsieur."

"Very well. Tell her to wait for me. Give her some supper. I'll see her in ten minutes."

When the man had disappeared my friend took me by the arm, saying: "Let us walk along slowly, while I tell you this story.

"Seven years ago, when I arrived here, I went out one evening to take a walk in the forest. It was a beautiful day, like to-day, and I was walking along slowly under the great trees, looking at the stars through the leaves, drinking in the quiet restfulness of night and the forest.

" I had just left Paris forever. I was tired out, more disgusted than I can say by all the foolish, low, and nasty things which I had seen and in which I had participated for fifteen years.

" I walked along for a great distance in this deep forest, following a path which leads to the village of Crouzille, about eight miles from here.

" Suddenly my dog, a great St. Bernard, which never left me, stopped short and began to growl. I thought that perhaps a fox, a wolf, or a boar might be in the neighborhood; I advanced gently on tip-toe, in order to make no noise, but suddenly I heard mournful, human cries, piercing yet muffled. I thought that surely some one was committing mur-der, and I rushed forward, taking a tight grip on my heavy oak cane, a regular club.

" I was coming nearer to the moans, which now became more distinct, but strangely muffled. One might have thought that, they were coming from some house, perhaps from the hut of some charcoal burner. Three feet ahead of me Bock was running, stopping, barking, starting again, very excited, and always growling. Suddenly another dog, a big black one with snapping eyes, barred our progress. I could clearly see his white fangs, which seemed to be shining in his mouth.

" I ran toward him with uplifted cane, but Bock had already jumped, and the two beasts were roll-ing around the ground with their teeth buried in each other. I went past them and almost bumped into a horse lying in the road. As I stopped, in surprise, to examine the animal, I saw in front of me a wagon, or, rather, a rolling house, such as are inhabited by gypsies and the traveling merchants who go from fair to fair.

" The cries were coming from there, frightful and continuous. As the door opened from the other side I turned around this vehicle and rushed up the three wooden steps, ready to jump on the malefactor.

" What I saw seemed so strange to me that I could at first understand nothing. A man was kneeling, and seemed to be praying, while in the bed something impossible to recognize, a half-naked creature, whose face I could not see, was moving, twisting about, and howling. It was a woman in labor.

" As soon as I understood the kind of an accident which was the cause of these screams, I made my presence known, and the man, wild with grief, begged me to save him, to save her, promising to me an unbelievable thankfulness. I had never seen a birth; I had never helped a female creature, woman, dog, or cat, in such a circumstance, and I said so as I foolishly watched this thing which was screaming so in the bed.

" Then I gathered my wits again, and I asked the grief-stricken man why he did not go to the next village. It seems that his horse had stepped into a rut and had broken part of his leg.

" ' Well, my man,' I exclaimed, ' there are two of us now, and we will drag your wife to my house.'

" But the howling dogs forced us to go outside, and we had to separate them by beating them with our sticks, at the risk of killing them. Then the idea struck me to harness them with us, one to the right and the other to the left, in order to help us. In ten minutes everything was ready, and the wagon started forward slowly, shaking the poor, suffering woman each time it would bump over a rut.

"Such a road, my friend! We were going along, panting, perspiring, slipping, and falling, while our poor dogs puffed along beside us.

"It took three hours to reach the cottage. When we arrived before the door the cries from the wagon had ceased. Mother and child were getting along well.

"They were put to bed, and then I had a horse harnessed up in order to go for a physician, while the man, an inhabitant of Marseilles, reassured,

consoled, glorying, was stuffing himself with food and getting drunk in order to celebrate this happy birth.

"It was a girl.

"I kept these people with me for a week. The mother, Mademoiselle Elmire, was an extraordinarily lucid somnambulist, who promised me an interminable life and countless joys.

"The following year, at exactly the same date, toward nightfall, the servant who has just called

me came to me in the smoking-room after dinner
and said: ' It's the gypsy of last yea. who has
come to thank Monsieur.'

" I had her come in the house, and I remained
dumfounded as I saw beside her a tall blond fellow, a man from the North, who bowed and spoke
to me as chief of the community. He had heard of
my kindness for Mademoiselle Elmire, and he had
not wished to let this anniversary go by without
bringing to me their thanks and a testimony of their
gratefulness.

" I gave them supper in the kitchen, and offered them my hospitality for the night. They left
the following day.

" The woman returns every year at the same
date with the child, a fine little girl, and a new
man  .  .  . each time. One man only, a fellow
from Auvergne, came back two years in succession.
The little girl calls them all ' Papa,' just as one says
' Monsieur ' with us."

We were arriving at the cottage, and we could
barely distinguish three shadows standing on the
porch, waiting for us. The tallest one took a few
steps forward, made a great bow, and said: '' Monsieur le Comte, we have come to-day in recognition
of our gratefulness.  .  .  .''

He was a Belgian!

After him, the little one spoke in the shrill, sing-
sing voice which children use when they recite a
composition.

I played ignorance, and I took Mademoiselle Elmire to the side, and, after a few questions, I asked
her: " Is that the father of your child? "

" Oh! no, Monsieur."

" Is the father dead? "

"Oh! no, Monsieur. We still see each other from time to time. He is a gendarme."

"What! then it wasn't the fellow from Marseilles who was there at the birth?"

"Oh! no, Monsieur. That was a rascal who stole all my savings."

"And the gendarme, the real father, does he know his child?"

"Oh! yes, Monsieur, and he loves her very much; but he can't take care of her because he has other ones from his wife."

# A Sale

HE defendants, Cé-saire - Isidore Bru-ment and Prosper Napoléon Cornu, appeared before the Court of Assizes of the Seine-Inférieure on a charge of attempted murder, by drowning, of Madame Brument, lawful wife of the first of the afore-named.

The two prisoners sat side by side on the traditional bench. They were two peasants; the first was small and stout, with short arms, short legs, and a round head, with a red, pimply face planted directly on his trunk, which was also round and short, and with apparently no neck. He was a raiser of pigs, and lived at Cacheville-la-Goupil, in the Canton of Criquetot.

Cornu (Prosper-Napoléon) was thin, of medium height, with enormously long arms. His head was on crooked, his jaw awry, and he squinted. A blue blouse, as long as a shirt, hung down to his knees, and his yellow hair, which was scanty and plastered down on his head, gave his face a worn-out, dirty look, a ruined look that was frightful. He had been nicknamed " the *curé*," because he could imitate to perfection the chanting in church and even the sound of the serpent. This talent attracted to his café—for he was a saloon keeper at Criquetot—a great many customers who preferred the " mass at Cornu " to the mass in church.

Madame Brument, seated on the witness bench, was a thin peasant woman, who seemed to be always asleep. She sat there motionless, her hands crossed on her knees, gazing fixedly before her with a stupid expression.

The Judge continued his interrogation:

" Well, then, Madame Brument, they came into your house and threw you into a barrel full of water. Tell us the details. Stand up."

She rose. She looked as tall as a flagpole, with her cap, which appeared like a white skull cap. She said, in a drawling tone:

" I was shelling beans. Just then they came in. I said to myself: ' What is the matter with them? They do not seem natural; they seem up to some mischief.' They watched me sideways, like this, especially Cornu, because he squints. I do not like to see them together, for they are two good-for-nothings when they are in company. I said: ' What do you want with me? ' They did not answer. I had a sort of mistrust——"

The defendant Brument interrupted the witness hastily, saying:

" I was full."

Then Cornu, turning toward his accomplice, said, in the deep tones of an organ:

"Say that we were both full, and you will be telling no lie."

The Judge, severely: "You mean by that you were both drunk?"

Brument: "There can be no question about it."

Cornu: "That might happen to any one."

The Judge, to the victim: "Continue your testimony, woman Brument."

"Well, Brument said to me, 'Do you wish to earn a hundred sous?' 'Yes,' I replied, 'seeing that a hundred sous are not picked up in a horse's tracks.' Then he said: 'Open your eyes and do as I do,' and he went to fetch the large empty barrel which is under the rain pipe in the corner, and he turned it over and brought it into my kitchen, and stuck it down in the middle of the floor, and then he said to me: 'Go and fetch water until it is full.'

"So I went to the pond with two pails and carried water, and still more water for an hour, seeing that the barrel was as large as a vat, saving your presence, Monsieur le Président.

"All this time Brument and Cornu were drinking a glass, and then another glass, and then another. They were finishing their drinks when I said to them: 'You are full, fuller than this barrel.' And Brument answered me: 'Do not worry; go on with your work; your turn will come; each one has his share.' I paid no attention to what he said, as he was full.

"When the barrel was full to the brim, I said: 'There, that's done.'

"And then Cornu gave me a hundred sous. Not

Brument, Cornu; it was Cornu gave them to me. And Brument said: ' Do you wish to earn a hundred sous more？' ' Yes,' I said, for I am not accustomed to presents like that. Then he said: ' Take off your clothes.'

" ' Take off my clothes？'

" ' Yes,' he said.

" ' How many shall I take off？'

" ' If it worries you at all, keep on your chemise, that won't bother us.'

" A hundred sous, that is a hundred sous, and I have to undress myself, but I did not fancy undressing before those two good-for-nothings. I took off my cap, and then my jacket, and then my skirt, and then my sabots. Brument said: ' Keep on your stockings, also; we are good fellows.'

" And Cornu said, too: ' We are good fellows.'

" So there I was, almost like Mother Eve. And they got up from their chairs, but could not stand straight, they were so full, saving your presence, Monsieur le Président.

" I said to myself: ' What are they up to？'

" And Brument said: ' Are you ready？'

" And Cornu said: ' I'm ready! '

" And then they took me, Brument by the head and Cornu by the feet, as one might take, for instance, a sheet that has been washed. Then I began to bawl.

" And Brument said: ' Keep still, wretched creature.'

" And they lifted me up in the air and put me into the barrel which was full of water, so that I had a check of the circulation, a chill to my very insides.

" And Brument said: ' Is that all？'

" Cornu said: ' That is all.'

" Brument said: ' The head is not in; that will make a difference in the measure.'

" Cornu said: ' Put in her head.'

" And then Brument pushed down my head as if to drown me, so that I could already see Paradise. And he pushed it down, and I disappeared.

" And then he must have been frightened. He pulled me out and said: ' Go and get dry, carcass.'

" As for me, I took to my heels and ran as far as Monsieur le curé's. He lent me a skirt belonging to his servant, for I was almost in a state of nature, and he went to fetch Maître Chicot, the country watchman, who went to Criquetot to fetch the police, who came to my house with me.

" There we found Brument and Cornu fighting each other like two rams.

" Brument was bawling: ' It isn't true; I tell you that there is at least a cubic meter in it. It is the method that was no good.'

" Cornu bawled: ' Four pails, that is almost half a cubic meter. You need not reply, that's what it is.'

" The police captain put them both under arrest. I have no more to tell."

She sat down. The audience in the courtroom laughed. The jurors looked at one another in astonishment. The judge said:

" Defendant Cornu, you seem to have been the instigator of this infamous plot. What have you to say? "

And Cornu rose in his turn.

" Judge," he replied, " I was full."

The Judge answered gravely:

"I know it. Proceed."

"I will. Well, Brument came to my place about nine o'clock, and ordered two drinks, and said: 'Here's one for you, Cornu.' I sat down opposite him and drank, and, out of politeness, I offered him a glass. Then he returned the compliment and so did I, and so it went on from glass to glass until noon, when we were full.

"Then Brument began to cry. That touched me. I asked him what was the matter. He said: 'I must have a thousand francs by Thursday.' That cooled me off a little, you understand. Then he said to me all at once: 'I will sell you my wife.'

"I was full, and I was a widower. You understand, that stirred me up. I did not know his wife, but she was a woman, wasn't she? I asked him: 'How much would you sell her for?'

"He reflected, or pretended to reflect. When one is full one is not very clear-headed, and he replied: 'I will sell her by the cubic meter.'

"That did not surprise me, for I was as drunk as he was, and I knew what a cubic meter is in my business. It is a thousand liters. That suited me.

"But the price remained to be settled. All depends on the quality. I said: 'How much do you want a cubic meter?'

"He answered: 'Two thousand francs.'

"I gave a bound like a rabbit, and then I reflected that a woman ought not to measure more than three hundred liters, so I said: 'That's too dear.'

"He answered: 'I cannot do it for less. I should lose by it.'

"You understand one is not a dealer in hogs for nothing. One understands one's business. But if he is smart, the seller of bacon, I am smarter, seeing that I sell them, also. Ha! ha! ha! So I said to him: ' If she were new I would not say anything, but she has been married to you for some time, so she is not as fresh as she was. I will give you fifteen hundred francs a cubic meter, not a sou more. Will that suit you?'

" He answered: ' That's a bargain!'

" I agreed, and we started out, arm in arm. We must help each other in this world.

" But a fear came to me: ' How can you measure her unless you put her into the liquid?'

" Then he explained his idea, not without difficulty, for he was full. He said to me: ' I take a barrel and fill it with water to the brim. I put her in it. All the water that comes out we will measure; that is the way to fix it.'

" I said: ' I see, I understand. But this water that overflows will run away; how are you going to gather it up?'

" Then he began stuffing me, and explained to me that all we should have to do would be to refill the barrel with the water his wife had displaced as soon as she should have left. All the water we should pour in would be the measure. I supposed about ten pails; that would be a cubic meter. He isn't a fool, all the same, when he is drunk, that old horse.

" To be brief, we reached his house, and I took a look at its mistress. A beautiful woman she certainly was not. Any one can see her, for there she is. I said to myself: ' I am disappointed, but never mind, she will be of value; handsome or ugly, it is all the same, is it not, Monsieur le Président?' And then I saw that she was as thin as a rail. I said to myself: ' She will not measure four hundred liters.' I understand the matter, it being in liquids.

" She told you about the proceeding. I even let her keep on her chemise and stockings, to my own disadvantage.

" When that was done she ran away. I said: ' Look out, Brument! she is escaping.'

" He replied: ' Do not be afraid, I will catch her, all right. She will have to come back to sleep. I will measure the deficit.'

" We measured. Not four pailfuls. Ha! ha! ha! "

The witness began to laugh so persistently that a gendarme was obliged to punch him in the back. Having quieted down, he resumed:

" In short, Brument exclaimed: ' Nothing doing; that is not enough.' I bawled and bawled, and bawled again, he punched me, I hit back. That would have kept on till the Day of Judgment, seeing we were both drunk.

" Then came the gendarmes! They swore at us, they took us off to prison. I want damages."

He sat down.

Brument confirmed in every particular the statements of his accomplice. The jury, in consternation, retired to deliberate.

At the end of an hour they returned a verdict of acquittal for the defendants, with some severe strictures on the dignity of marriage, and establishing the precise limitations of business transactions.

Brument went home to the domestic roof accompanied by his wife.

Cornu went back to his business.

## Our English Neighbors

 LITTLE bound notebook lay on the cushioned seat of the railway carriage. I took it up and opened it. It was a diary of travel, lost by some traveler:

I copy here the last three pages:

*February 1.* Mentone, chief city of consumptives, celebrated for its pulmonary tubercles. Very different from the tubercle of the sweet potato, which lives and germinates in the earth to nourish and fatten human beings, this species of vegetation lives and germinates in man to nourish and enrich the soil.

I got this scientific definition from a kind and learned physician of the district.

I am looking for a hotel; I am directed to the gr-r-r-eat Hôtel de Russie, d'Angleterre, et des Pays-Bas.

With great respect for the cosmopolitan intelligence of the proprietor, I take a room in this hospital, which seems to me to be empty, it is so large.

Then I take a walk round the town, which is pretty and pleasantly situated at the foot of an imposing mountain (see the guide-books). I meet people who have a sickly appearance being led about by others who look bored. Here one meets many mufflers. (This is for naturalists, who might be troubled at their disappearance.)

Six o'clock. I come home to dinner. The table was laid in a vast dining-room, which was intended for three hundred guests, but which at present shelters exactly twenty-two. They come in one after another. First comes a tall Englishman, close-shaven and thin, with a long, tight-fitting frock-coat, the sleeves of which confine his thin arms as an umbrella sheath covers an umbrella. This garment, which recalled the civilian uniform of old army captains, the dress of invalided veterans, and the cassock of priests, was ornamented down the front with a row of black cloth buttons, placed close to each other like a battalion of wood-lice. On the opposite side was a row of buttonholes.

The waistcoat was fastened in the same manner. The owner of this suit does not appear to be humorous.

He bows to me. I return his politeness.

Second entry. Three ladies, Englishwomen, a mother and two daughters. Each wears on her head what looks like a beaten egg, which astonishes me. The daughters are as old as the mother, the mother is as old as the daughters. They are all three thin, with flat figures, tall, slow, and stiff, and they show their teeth to inspire men and food with fear.

Other guests enter, all English. One of them alone is big and red-faced, with white whiskers. Every woman (there are fourteen) wears on her head a beaten egg. I perceive that this *entremet* headdress is made of white lace or foamy tulle, I do not know which. It does not appear to be sweetened. All these ladies appear to have been preserved in vinegar, although there are five young girls among them, not bad-looking, but hopelessly flat-figured.

I recall Bouilhet's lines:

> " *Qu' importe ton sein maigre, ô mon objet aimé?*
> *On est plus près du cœur quand la poitrine est plate,*
> *Et je vois, comme un merle en sa cage enfermé,*
> *L' amour entre tes os, rêvant sur une patte."*

Two young men, younger than the first, are also inclosed in priestly frock-coats. They are lay brothers, with wives and children, called pastors. They look cleaner, more serious, and less amiable than our priests. I would not exchange a ton of these for a barrel of those. Every one to his taste.

As soon as the guests were all in the head pastor took the floor and pronounced in English a sort of very long *Bénédicité*, to which every one at table listened with a penitent air.

The food being thus consecrated, in spite of myself, to the God of Israel and of Albion, every one began to eat his soup.

A solemn silence reigned in the spacious dining-room, a silence that could not be normal. I suppose my presence is disagreeable to this colony, into which no tainted sheep had entered hitherto.

The women, in particular, have an appearance of stiffness and restraint, as if they feared that their little headdress of beaten egg might fall into their plates.

However, the head pastor addressed a few words to his neighbor, the assistant pastor. As I have the misfortune to understand a little English, I noticed with astonishment that they were resuming a conversation that had been interrupted before dinner, on the sayings of the prophets.

Every one listened reflectively.

Then they fed me, still in spite of myself, on incredible quotations.

" I will pour out water for him that is thirsty," said Isaiah.

I knew nothing about it. I also knew nothing about all the truths uttered by Jeremiah, Malachi, Ezekiel, etc.

They entered my ears like flies, these simple truths, and buzzed in my brain.

" Let him that hungers ask bread."

" The air belongs to the birds as the sea belongs to the fishes."

" The fig tree yields figs and the palm dates."

" The man who does not heed will not obtain wisdom."

How much grander and deeper is our great Henri Monnier, who makes one man, the immortal Prud'homme, utter more brilliant truths than all the prophets combined!

He cries on seeing the ocean: " The ocean is beautiful, but what a waste of land! "

He formulates the eternal policy of the world: " This sword is the most beautiful day of my life. I shall know how to use it to protect the Power that gives it to me, and, if necessary, to attack it."

If I had had the honor to be introduced to the

company of English people by whom I was surrounded, I should assuredly have edified them with
selected quotations from our French prophet.

When dinner was over we went into the drawing-
room.

I sat alone in a corner. The British tribe seemed
to be conspiring at the other end of the spacious room. Suddenly, a lady moved toward the
piano.

" Ah! a little music," I thought; " so much the
better."

She opened the instrument, sat down before it,
and all the colony surrounded her like a battalion,
the women on the inside and the men standing behind them.

Are they about to sing an opera?

The head pastor, now become leader of the choir,
raised his hand, then lowered it, and a nameless,
frightful clamor escaped from all these mouths,
which were singing a hymn.

The women squalled, the men roared, the windows shook. The hotel dog began to howl out in
the yard and was answered by another in one of the
rooms.

I fled, terrified, furious, and went for a walk
through the town. Not finding any theater, or
casino, or place of amusement, I had to come home
again.

The English were still singing.

I went to bed. They kept on singing. They
sang until midnight the praise of the Lord with the
most discordant, screeching, odious voices I ever
heard; while I, possessed by that horrible spirit of
mimicry which led away an entire people in a dance
of death, was humming beneath the sheets:

> "I am sorry for the Lord, the Lord God of Albion,
>    Whose glory they are singing in the parlor.
>        If the Lord has more ear
>        Than his faithful people,
>        If he loves talent, beauty,
>        Grace, wit, mirth,
> Excellent mimicry and good music, I pity the Lord with all
>    my heart!"

And when at last I was able to sleep, I had frightful nightmare. I saw prophets riding on the backs of the pastors and eating beaten eggs on the heads of corpses.

Horror! Horror!

*February 2.* As soon as I rose I asked the proprietor whether these barbarians, who had invaded his hotel, renewed their frightful amusement each day.

He answered, smiling:

"Oh, no, Monsieur; yesterday was Sunday, and you know that with them Sunday is sacred."

I replied:

> "Nothing is sacred for a pastor,
>    Neither the sleep of a traveler,
>    Nor his dinner, nor his ear.
>    But see to it that a similar thing
>    Does not occur again,
>    Or without hesitation
>    I shall take the train."

A little surprised, the proprietor promised that he would keep a lookout.

I took a very pretty walk on the mountainside during the course of the day.

When evening came I even took part in the *Bénédicité.* Then I went into the drawing-room.

What are they about to do? For a whole hour they did nothing. Suddenly, the same lady who played the accompaniment for the hymns the preceding evening moved toward the piano and opened it. I trembled with fear. She began to play—a waltz!

And the young girls began to dance.

The head pastor beat time on his knee from long habit. The Englishmen asked the ladies to dance, and the beaten eggs turned round and round and round like whirling dervishes.

I enjoyed that more than hymns. After the waltz came a quadrille and a polka.

Not having been introduced, I remained sequestered in a corner.

*February 3.* Another pretty walk to the old Castelar, a charming ruin on the mountain, which has remains of fortresses on all its summits.

There is nothing so beautiful as these ruins of strongholds amid the chaos of rocks which command the Alpine snows (see guide-book). This country is delightful.

During the dinner I introduced myself, French fashion, to my neighbor. She did not make any reply—English politeness!

In the evening they had an English ball.

*February 4.* Excursion to Monaco (see guide-book).

In the evening an English ball at which I took part, and was treated as if I carried infection.

*February 5.* Excursion to San Remo (see guide-book). Evening—English ball. My quarantine continues.

*February 6.* Excursion to Nice (see guide-book). Evening—English ball. I went to bed.

*February 7.* Excursion to Cannes (see guide-

book).  Evening—English ball.  I drank a cup of
tea in my corner.

*February 8.*   Sunday, grand revenge.  I was
waiting for them, the upstarts!

They had resumed their penitent Sunday air and
were preparing their voices to sing hymns.

Now, before dinner, I slipped into the drawing-
room, took the key of the piano and put it in my
pocket, and said to the office clerk:

" If the parsons ask for the key tell them that I
took it, and ask them to come and see me."

During dinner they discussed several disputed
Scriptural passages, explained texts, and cleared up
the genealogies of biblical personages.

Then they went into the drawing-room and
walked over to the piano.  Consternation!

They take counsel together.  The tribe seems
cast down.  The beaten eggs seem ready to fly
away.  At length the head pastor leaves the room
and presently returns.  They discuss the matter
and look at me with indignant eyes; and then the
three pastors move in my direction, one behind another, like ambassadors.  They look quite imposing.

They bow to me.  I rise from my seat.  The
oldest of them addresses me:

" Monsieur, they tell me that you have taken the
key of the piano.  The ladies would like to have it
so that they can sing hymns."

I replied:

" Monsieur l'Abbé, I understand perfectly the
request of these ladies; but I cannot grant it.  You
are a religious man, Monsieur, and so am I, and my
principles, doubtless more strict than your own,
have decided me to prevent the profanation to which
you are yielding yourselves.

" I cannot permit, gentlemen, that you should employ, in order to sing to the glory of God, an instrument that has been used all the week to make young girls dance. We do not give public balls in our churches, Monsieur, and we do not play quadrilles on organs. The use to which you put the piano angers and shocks me. You may take my reply to the ladies."

The three pastors retired in dismay. The ladies appeared amazed. And they began to sing hymns without the piano.

*February 9.* Noon. The hotel proprietor came to ask me to leave. They are expelling me at the general request of the English.

I met the three pastors, who seemed to be superintending my departure. I went straight up to them. I bowed.

" Gentlemen," I said, " you seem to be very well informed on the subject of the Scriptures. Personally I have given quite a little study to these subjects. I even know a little Hebrew. Now, I should like to submit to you a matter that troubles my Catholic conscience very much."

And, after shocking them with a *résumé* of some biblical genealogies, I declared it was scandalous to make us read ten pages of genealogy at dessert.

" We spoil our eyes in order to learn that A . . . begat B . . ., who begat C . . ., who begat D . . ., who begat E . . ., who begat F . . ., and when we are almost crazy from this interminable list, we arrive at the last, who begat nobody. We may call that, gentlemen, the acme of mystification ! "

The three pastors abruptly turned their backs on me as one man and fled.

Two o'clock. I am taking the train for Nice.

The journal ends here. Although these notes show extremely bad taste, a common mind, and much coarseness, I thought that they might put certain travelers on their guard against the danger from English tourists.

I must add that there are charming English people; I know some, and many of them. But as a rule they are not those we meet in hotels.

# Timbuctoo

THE boulevard, that river of humanity, was alive with people in the golden light of the setting sun. The whole sky was red, blinding; and behind the Madeleine a great bank of flaming clouds cast a shower of light the whole length of the boulevard, vibrant as the heat from a brazier.

The gay, animated crowd went by in this golden mist, and seemed to be glorified. Their faces were gilded, their black hats and clothes took on purple tints, the reflections on the asphalt of the sidewalk. patent leather of their shoes cast bright

Before the cafés a mass of men were drinking opalescent liquids that looked like precious stones dissolved in the glasses.

In the midst of the drinkers two officers in full uniform dazzled all eyes with their glittering gold lace. They chatted, happy without asking why, in this glory of life, in this radiant light of sunset, and they looked at the crowd, the leisurely men and the hurrying women, who left a bewildering odor of perfume as they passed by.

All at once an enormous negro, dressed in black, with a paunch beneath his jean waistcoat, which was covered with charms, his face shining as if it had been polished, passed before them with a triumphant air. He laughed at the passers-by, at the news vendors, at the dazzling sky, at the whole of Paris. He was so tall that he overtopped every one else, and when he passed all the loungers turned round to look at his back.

But he suddenly perceived the officers, and darted toward them, jostling the drinkers in his path. As soon as he reached their table he fixed his gleaming and delighted eyes upon them, and the corners of his mouth expanded to his ears, showing his dazzling white teeth like a crescent moon in a black sky. The two men looked in astonishment at this ebony giant, unable to understand his delight.

With a voice that made all the guests laugh, he said:

"Good day, my Lieutenant."

One of the officers was commander of a battalion, the other was a colonel. The former said:

"I do not know you, sir; I am at a loss to know what you want of me."

"We like you much, Lieutenant Védié, siege of Bézi, much grapes, find me."

The officer, utterly bewildered, looked at the man intently, trying to refresh his memory; then he cried abruptly:

"Timbuctoo?"

The negro, radiant, slapped his thigh as he uttered a tremendous laugh and roared:

" Yes, yes, my Lieutenant, you remember Timbuctoo! Ya, how do you do? "

The commandant held out his hand, laughing heartily as he did so. Then Timbuctoo became serious. He seized the officer's hand, and, before the other could prevent it, he kissed it, according to negro and Arab custom. The officer, embarrassed, said in a severe tone:

" Come, now, Timbuctoo, we are not in Africa. Sit down there and tell me how it is I find you here."

Timbuctoo swelled himself out and, his words falling over one another, replied hurriedly:

" I make much money, much, big restaurant, good food, Prussians, me much steal, much, French cooking, Timbuctoo, cook to the Emperor, two thousand francs mine. Ha! ha! ha! ha! "

And he laughed, doubling himself up, roaring, with wild delight in his glances.

When the officer, who understood his strange manner of expressing himself, had questioned him, he said:

" Well, *au revoir*, Timbuctoo. I will see you again."

The negro rose, this time shaking the hand that was extended to him, and, smiling still, cried:

" Good day, good day, my Lieutenant! "

He went off, so happy that he gesticulated as he walked, and people thought he was crazy.

" Who is that brute? " asked the Colonel.

" A fine fellow and a brave soldier. I will tell you what I know about him. It is funny enough.

" You know that at the beginning of the war

of 1870 I was shut up in Bezières, which this negro called Bézi. We were not besieged, but blockaded. The Prussian lines surrounded us on all sides, outside the reach of cannon, not firing on us, but slowly starving us out.

" I was then lieutenant. Our garrison consisted of all descriptions of soldiers, fragments of slaughtered regiments, some that had run away, and freebooters separated from the main army. We had all kinds—in fact, even eleven—Turcos (Algerian soldiers in the service of France), who arrived one evening no one knew whence or how. They appeared at the gates of the city, exhausted, in rags, starving and dirty. They were handed over to me.

" I saw very soon that they were absolutely undisciplined, always in the street, and always drunk. I tried putting them in the police station, even in prison, but nothing was of any use. They would disappear, sometimes for days at a time, as if they had been swallowed up by the earth, and then come back staggering drunk. They had no money. Where did they buy drink? And how, and with what?

" This began to worry me greatly, all the more as these savages interested me with their everlasting laugh and their characteristics of overgrown, frolicsome children.

" I then noticed that they blindly obeyed the largest among them, the one you have just seen. He made them do as he pleased, and planned their mysterious expeditions with the all-powerful and undisputed authority of a leader. I sent for him and questioned him. Our conversation lasted fully three hours, for it was hard for me to understand his remarkable gibberish. As for him, poor devil, he made unheard-of efforts to make himself intelligible, invented words, gesticulated, perspired in his anxiety, mopping his forehead, puffing, stopping, and abruptly beginning again when he thought he had formed a new method of explaining what he wanted to say.

" I gathered, finally, that he was the son of a big chief, a sort of negro king of the region around Timbuctoo. I asked his name. He repeated something like *Chavaharibouhalikranapotapolara.* It seemed simpler to me to give him the name of his native place, Timbuctoo. And a week later he was known by no other name in the garrison.

" But we were all wildly anxious to find out where this African ex-prince procured his drinks. I discovered it in a singular manner.

" I was on the ramparts one morning, watching the horizon, when I perceived something moving about in a vineyard. It was near the time of vintage, the grapes were ripe, but I was not thinking of that. I thought that a spy was approaching the town, and I organized a complete expedition to catch the prowler. I took command myself, after obtaining permission from the general.

" I sent out by three different gates three little companies, which were to meet at the suspected vineyard and form a cordon round it. In order to cut off the spy's retreat one of these detachments had to make at least an hour's march. A watch on the walls signaled to me that the person I had seen had not left the place. We went along in profound silence, creeping, almost crawling along the paths. At last we reached the spot assigned.

" I abruptly disbanded my soldiers, who darted

into the vineyard, and found—Timbuctoo, on hands and knees, traveling round among the vines and eating grapes, or, rather, devouring them as a dog eats his sop, snatching them in mouthfuls from the vine with his teeth.

" I wanted him to get up, but he could not think of it. I then understood why he was crawling on his hands and knees. As soon as we stood him on his feet he began to wabble, then stretched out his arms and fell down on his nose. He was more drunk than I have ever seen any one.

" They brought him home on two poles. He never stopped laughing all the way back, while gesticulating with his arms and legs.

" This explained the mystery. My men also drank the juice of the grapes, and when they were so intoxicated they could not stir, they went to sleep in the vineyard. As for Timbuctoo, his love of the vineyard was beyond all belief and all bounds. He lived in it as did the thrushes, which he hated with the jealous hatred of a rival. He repeated incessantly:

" ' The thrushes eat all the grapes, Captain! '

" One evening I was sent for. Something had been seen on the plain coming in our direction. I had not brought my field-glass, and I could not distinguish things clearly. It looked like a great serpent uncoiling itself—a convoy, how could I tell?

" I sent some men to meet this strange caravan, which presently made its triumphal entry. Timbuctoo and nine of his comrades were carrying, on a sort of altar made of camp stools, eight severed, grinning and bleeding heads. The African was dragging along a horse to whose tail another head was fastened, and six other animals followed, adorned in the same manner.

"This is what I learned. Having set out for the vineyard, my Africans had suddenly perceived a detachment of Prussians approaching a village. Instead of taking to their heels they hid themselves, and as soon as the Prussian officers dismounted at an inn to refresh themselves, the eleven rascals rushed on them, put to flight the lancers, who thought they were being attacked by the main army, killed the two sentries, then the Colonel and the five officers of his escort.

"That day I kissed Timbuctoo. I saw, however, that he walked with difficulty, and thought he was wounded. He laughed and said:

"'Me, provisions for my country.'

"Timbuctoo was not fighting for glory, but for gain. Everything he found that seemed to him to be of the slightest value, especially anything that glistened, he put in his pocket. What a pocket! An abyss that began at his hips and reached to his ankles. He had retained an old term used by the troopers, and called it his *profonde,* and it was his *profonde,* in fact!

"He had taken the gold lace off the Prussian uniforms, the brass off their helmets, detached their buttons, and had thrown them all into his *profonde,* which was full to overflowing.

"Each day he pocketed every glistening object that came to his observation: pieces of tin or pieces of silver, and sometimes his contour was very comical.

"He intended to carry all that back to the land of ostriches, whose brother he might have been, this son of a king, tormented with the longing to gobble up all objects that glistened. If he had not had his *profonde,* what would he have done? Doubtless he would have swallowed them.

" Every morning his pocket was empty. He had, then, some general store where his riches were piled up. But where? I could not discover it.

" The General, on being informed of Timbuc-too's mighty act of valor, had the headless bodies that had been left in the neighboring village interred at once, that it might not be discovered that they were decapitated. The Prussians returned thither the following day. The Mayor and seven prominent inhabitants were shot on the spot, by way of reprisal, as having denounced the Prussians.

" Winter arrived. We were exhausted and desperate. There were skirmishes every day. The famished men could no longer march. The eight ' Turcos ' alone (three had been killed) remained fat, shiny, vigorous, and always ready to fight. Timbuctoo was even getting fatter. He said to me one day:

" ' You, much hungry, me good meat.'

" And he brought me an excellent *filet.* But of what? We had no more cattle, nor sheep, nor goats, nor donkeys, nor pigs. It was impossible to find a horse. I thought of all this after I had devoured my meat. Then a horrible idea came to me. These negroes were born close to a country where they eat human beings! And each day such a number of soldiers were killed around the town. I questioned Timbuctoo. He would not answer. I did not insist, but from that time I declined his presents.

" He worshiped me. One night snow took us by surprise at the outposts. We were seated on the ground. I looked with pity at those poor negroes, shivering beneath the white, frozen shower. I was very cold and began to cough. At once I felt something fall on me, like a large warm quilt. It was Timbuctoo's cape, which he had thrown on my shoulders.

" I rose and returned his garment, saying:

" ' Keep it, my boy; you need it more than I.'

" ' No, my Lieutenant, for you; me no need, me hot, hot! '

" And he looked at me entreatingly.

" ' Come, obey orders! Keep your cape. I insist,' I repeated.

" He stood up, drew his sword, which he had sharpened to an edge like a scythe, and, holding in his other hand the large cape which I had refused, said:

" ' If you not keep cape, me cut; no one cape.'

" And he would have done it. So I yielded.

" Eight days later we capitulated. Some of us had been able to escape. The rest were to march out of the town and give themselves up to the conquerors.

" I went toward the exercising-ground, where we were all to meet, when I was dumfounded at the sight of a gigantic negro dressed in white duck and wearing a straw hat. It was Timbuctoo. He was beaming and was walking with his hands in his pockets, in front of a little shop where two plates and two glasses were displayed.

" ' What are you doing? ' I asked.

" ' Me not go, me good cook, me make food for Colonel, Algeria; me eat P'ussians, much steal, much.'

" There were ten degrees of frost. I shivered

at sight of this negro in white duck. He took me by the arm and made me go inside. I noticed a large flag that he intended to place outside his door as soon as we had left, for he had some shame. I read this sign, traced by the hand of some accomplice:

" ' Army kitchen of M. Timbuctoo,
" ' Formerly cook to H. M. the Emperor.
" ' *A Parisian Artist!    Moderate Prices.*'

" In spite of the despair that was gnawing at my heart, I could not help laughing, and I left my negro to his new enterprise.

" Was not that better than taking him prisoner?

" You have just seen that he made a success of it, the rascal.

" Bezières to-day belongs to the Germans. The Restaurant Timbuctoo is the beginning of a retaliation."

## The Effeminates

OW often we hear people say:
" He is charming, that man,
but he is a girl, a regular
girl." They are alluding to
the girl-man, the bane of our
land.

For we are all girl-men
in France—that is, fickle,
fanciful, innocently treacherous, without consistency
in our convictions or our
will; violent and weak as women are.

But the most irritating of girl-men is assuredly
the Parisian and the *boulevardier,* in whom the appearance of intelligence is more marked, and who
combines in himself all the attractions and all the
faults of those charming creatures in an exagger-
ated degree in virtue of his masculine temperament.

Our Chamber of Deputies is full of girl-men.
They form the greater number of the amiable op-
portunists whom one might call " the charmers."

These are they who control by soft words and deceitful promises, who know how to shake hands in such a manner as to win hearts; how to say " My dear friend " in a certain tactful way to persons they know the least; to change their mind without suspecting it; to be carried away by each new idea; to be sincere in their weathercock convictions; to let themselves be deceived as they deceive others; to forget the next morning what they affirmed the day before.

The newspapers are full of these effeminate men. That is probably where one finds the most of them, but it is also where they are most needed. The *Journal des Débats* and the *Gazette de France* are exceptions.

Assuredly, every good journalist must be somewhat effeminate, that is, at the command of the public, supple in following unconsciously the shades of public opinion, wavering and varying, skeptical and credulous, wicked and devout, a braggart and a true man, enthusiastic and ironical, and always appearing to be convinced while believing in nothing.

Foreigners, our antitypes, as Madame Abel called them, the stubborn English and the heavy Germans, regard us with a certain amazement, mingled with contempt, and will continue so to regard us till the end of time. They consider us frivolous. It is not that; it is that we are girls. And that is the reason why people love us in spite of our faults, why they come back to us despite the evil spoken of us; these are mere lovers' quarrels!

The effeminate man, as one meets him in the world, is so charming that he captivates you after five minutes' chat. His smile seems made for you; one cannot believe that his voice does not assume

specially tender intonations on his hearer's account.
When he leaves it seems as if one had known him
for twenty years. One is quite ready to lend him
money should he ask for it. He has enchanted you,
like a woman.

If he commits any breach of manners toward
you, you cannot bear any malice, he is so pleasant
when you next meet him. If he asks your pardon,
you long to ask pardon of him! Does he tell lies?
You cannot believe it. Does he put you off indefinitely with promises that he does not keep? One re-
lies upon his promises as if he had moved heaven
and earth to render a service.

When he admires anything he goes into such
raptures that he convinces you. He once adored
Victor Hugo, whom he now treats as an antiquity.
He would have fought for Zola, whom he has abandoned for Barbey d'Aurevilly. And when he admires he permits no limitation, he would slap your
face for a word. But when he becomes scornful
his contempt is unbounded and allows no protest.

In fact, he understands nothing.

Listen to two girls talking:

" Then you are angry with Julia? "

" I slapped her face."

" What had she done? "

" She told Pauline that I had no money thirteen
months out of twelve. And Pauline told Gontran—
you understand."

" You were living together in the Rue Clau-
zel? "

" We lived together four years ago in the Rue
Bréda. We quarreled about a pair of stockings that
she said I had worn—it wasn't true—silk stockings
that she had bought at Mother Martin's. Then I

gave her a pounding and she left me at once. I met her six months ago, and she asked me to come and live with her, as she has rented a flat that is twice too large.''

One goes his way and hears no more. But on the following Sunday, as he is on the way to Saint-Germain, two young women enter the same railway carriage. He recognizes one of them at once; it is Julia's enemy. The other is—Julia!

And there are endearments, caresses, plans. '' Now, Julia—listen, Julia,'' and so on.

The girl-man has friendships of this kind. For three months he cannot bear to leave his old Jack, his dear Jack. There is no one but Jack in the world. He is the only one who has any intelligence, any sense, any talent. He alone amounts to anything in Paris. One meets them everywhere together; they dine together, walk about in company, and every evening walk home with each other, back and forth, without being able to part.

Three months later, if Jack is mentioned, we hear:

'' There is a drinker, a sorry fellow, a scoundrel for you! I knew him well, you may be sure. He is not even honest; he is ill-bred,'' etc., etc.

Three months later they are living together! But one morning one hears that they have fought a duel, then embraced each other amid tears on the dueling ground.

Just now they are the dearest friends in the world, furious with each other half the year, abusing and loving each other by turns, squeezing each other's hands till they almost crush the bones, and ready to run each other through the body for a misunderstanding.

For the relations of these effeminate men are uncertain. Their temper comes by fits and starts; their delight is unexpected; their affection fluctuates; their enthusiasm is subject to eclipse. One day they love you, the next day they will hardly look at you, for they have, in fact, a girl's nature, a girl's charm, a girl's temperament, and all their sentiments are like the affection of girls.

They treat their friends as women treat their pet dogs.

It is the dear little *tonton,* whom they hug, feed with sugar, allow to sleep on the pillow, but which they would be just as likely to throw out of the window in a moment of impatience, which they turn round like a sling, holding it by the tail, squeeze in their arms till they almost strangle it, and plunge without any reason into a pail of cold water.

Then what a strange thing it is when one of these beings falls in love with a real girl! He beats her; she scratches him; they execrate each other, cannot bear the sight of each other, and yet cannot part, linked together by no one knows what mysterious psychic bonds. She deceives him; he knows it, sobs, and forgives her. He despises and adores her, without seeing that she would be justified in despising him. They are both atrociously unhappy and yet cannot separate. They cast invectives, reproaches, and abominable accusations at each other from morning till night; and when they have reached the climax, and are vibrating with rage and hatred, they fall into each other's arms and kiss each other ardently.

The girl-man is brave and a coward at the same time. He has more than another the exalted sentiment of honor, but is lacking in the sense of simple honesty, and, circumstances favoring him, would defalcate and commit infamies which do not trouble his conscience, for he obeys, without questioning, the oscillation of his ideas, which are always impulsive.

To him it seems permissible and almost right to cheat a haberdasher. He does not consider it dishonorable not to pay his debts, unless they are gambling debts. He dupes people whenever the laws of society admit of his doing so. When he is short of money he borrows in all ways, not always being scrupulous as to tricking the lenders, but he would with sincere indignation run his sword through any one who should suspect him only of lacking in delicacy or politeness.

# The Mustache

CHÂTEAU DE SOLLES,

July 30, 1883.

Y DEAR LUCY: I have no news. We live in the drawing-room, looking out at the rain. We cannot go out in this frightful weather, so we have theatricals. How stupid they are, my dear, these drawing-room entertainments in the repertory of real life! All is forced, coarse, heavy. The jokes are like cannon-balls, smashing everything in their passage. No wit, nothing natural, no sprightliness, no elegance. These literary men, in truth, know nothing of society. They are perfectly ignorant of how people think and talk in our set. I do not mind if they despise our customs, our conventionalities, but I do not forgive them for not knowing them. When they wish to be humorous they make puns that would do for a barrack; when they try

to be jolly they give us jokes that they must have picked up on the outer boulevard, in those beer-houses that artists are supposed to frequent, where one has heard the same students' jokes for fifty years.

So we have taken to theatricals. As we are only two women, my husband takes the part of a soubrette, and, in order to do that, he has shaved off his mustache. You cannot imagine, my dear Lucy, how it changes him! I no longer recognize him—by day or at night. If he did not let it grow again I think I should no longer love him, he looks so horrid like this.

In fact, a man without a mustache is no longer a man. I do not care much for a beard; it almost always makes a man look untidy. But a mustache —oh, a mustache is indispensable to a manly face! No, you never would believe how those little bristles on the upper lip are a relief to the eye and good in other ways. I have thought over the matter a great deal, but hardly dare to write my thoughts. Words look so different on paper, and the subject is so difficult, so delicate, so dangerous, that it requires infinite skill to broach it.

Well, when my husband appeared shaven, I understood at once that I never could fall in love with a strolling actor nor a preacher, even if it were Father Didon, the most charming of all! Later, when I was alone with him (my husband) it was worse still. Oh, my dear Lucy, never let yourself be kissed by a man without a mustache; their kisses have no flavor, none whatever! They no longer have the charm, the mellowness, and the—yes, the piquancy of a real kiss. The mustache lends the spice.

Imagine placing to your lips a piece of dry—
or moist—parchment. That is the kiss of the man
without a mustache. It is not worth while.

Whence comes this charm of the mustache, will
you tell me? Do I know myself? It tickles your
face, you feel it approaching your mouth, and it
sends a little shiver through you down to the tips
of your toes.

And on your neck! Have you ever felt a mustache on your neck? It intoxicates you, makes you
feel creepy, goes to the tips of your fingers. You
wriggle, shake your shoulders, toss back your head.
You wish to get away and at the same time to remain there; it is delightful, but irritating. But how
sweet it is!

A lip without a mustache is like a body without clothing; and one must wear clothes—very few,
if you like—but still some clothing.

I recall a sentence (uttered by a politician) which
has been running in my mind for three months.
My husband, who keeps up with the newspapers,
read me one evening a very singular speech by our
Minister of Agriculture, who was called M. Méline.
He may have been superseded by this time—I do
not know.

I was paying no attention, but the name, Méline,
struck me. It recalled, I do not exactly know why,
the *Scènes de la Vie de Bohème.* I thought it was
about some grisette. That shows how scraps of
the speech entered my mind. This M. Méline was
making this statement to the people of Amiens, I
believe, and I have ever since been trying to understand what he meant: "There is no patriotism
without agriculture!" Well, I have just discovered his meaning; and I affirm in my turn that there

is no love without a mustache. When you say it
that way it sounds comical, does it not?

There is no love without a mustache!

"There is no patriotism without agriculture,"
said M. Méline, and he was right, that Minister. I
now understand why.

From a very different point of view, the mustache is essential. It gives character to the face.
It makes a man look gentle or tender, violent or a
monster, a rake or enterprising! The hairy man
who does not shave his beard never has a refined
look, for his features are concealed; and the shape
of the jaw and the chin betray a great deal to those
who understand.

The man with a mustache retains his own peculiar expression and his refinement.

And how many different varieties of mustaches
there are! Sometimes they are twisted, curled,
coquettish. Those seem to be devoted chiefly to
women.

Sometimes they are pointed, sharp as needles,
and threatening. That kind prefers wine, horses,
and war.

Sometimes they are enormous, overhanging,
frightful. These big ones usually conceal a fine
disposition, a kindliness that borders on weakness,
and a gentleness that savors of timidity.

But what I adore above all in the mustache is
the fact that it is French, altogether French. It
came from our ancestors, the Gauls, and has remained the insignia of our national character.

It is boastful, gallant, and brave. It sips wine
gracefully and knows how to laugh with refinement;
while the broad, bearded jaws are clumsy in everything they do.

I recall something that made me weep bitter tears, and also—I see it now—made me love a mustache on a man's face.

It was during the war, when I was living with my father. I was a young girl then. One day there was a skirmish near the château. I had heard the firing of cannon and artillery all the morning, and that evening a German colonel came and took up his abode in our house. He left the following day. My father was informed that there were several dead bodies in the fields. He had them brought to our place so that they might be buried together. They were laid all along the great avenue of pines as fast as they brought them in, on both sides of the avenue, and as they began to smell unpleasant their bodies were covered with earth until the deep trench could be dug. Thus one saw only their heads, which seemed to protrude from the clayed earth and were almost as yellow, with their closed eyes.

I wanted to see them. But when I saw those two rows of frightful faces I thought I should faint. However, I began to look at them, one by one, trying to guess what kind of men these had been.

The uniforms were concealed beneath the earth, and yet, immediately, yes, immediately, my dear, I recognized the Frenchmen by their mustaches!

Some of them had shaved on the very day of the battle, as if they wished to be elegant up to the last; others seemed to have a week's growth; but all wore the French mustache, very plain, the proud mustache that seems to say: " Do not take me for my bearded friend, little one; I am a brother."

And I cried, oh, I cried a great deal more than

I should if I had not recognized them, the poor dead fellows!

It is wrong of me to tell you this. Now, I am sad and cannot chatter any longer. Well, good-by, dear Lucy; I send you a hearty kiss. Long live the mustache!

JEANNE.

## A Stroll

WHEN Old Man Leras, bookkeeper for Messieurs Labuze and Company, left the store, he stood for a minute bewildered at the glory of the setting sun. He had worked all day in the yellow light of a small jet of gas, far in the back of the store, on a narrow court, as deep as a well. The little room where he had been spending his days for forty years was so dark that even in the middle of summer one could only go without the gaslight from eleven until three.

It was always damp and cold, and from this hole on which his window opened came the musty odor of a sewer.

For forty years Monsieur Leras had been arriving every morning in this prison at eight o'clock, and he would remain there until seven at night, bending over his books, writing with the application of a good clerk.

He was now making three thousand francs a year, having started at fifteen hundred. He had remained a bachelor, as his means had not allowed him the luxury of a wife, and as he had never enjoyed anything, he desired nothing. From time to time, however, tired of his continuous and monotonous work, he formed a platonic wish: '' Gad! If I only had an income of fifteen thousand francs, I would take life easy.''

He had never taken life easy, as he had never had anything but his monthly salary. His life had been uneventful, without emotions, without hopes. The faculty of dreaming with which every one is blessed had never developed in the mediocrity of his ambitions.

When he was twenty-one he entered the employ of Messieurs Labuze and Company. And he had never left them.

In 1856 he had lost his father, and then his mother in 1859. Since then the only incident in his life was when he moved, in 1868, because his landlord had tried to raise his rent.

Every day his alarm clock made him jump out of bed at exactly six, with a frightful noise of rattling chains.

Twice, however, this piece of mechanism had been out of order. Once in 1866 and again in 1874; he had never been able to find out the reason why. He would dress, make his bed, sweep his room, dust his chair and the top of his bureau. All this took him an hour and a half.

Then he would go out, buy a roll at the Lahure Bakery, in which he had seen eleven different owners without the name ever changing, and he would eat this roll on the way to the office.

His entire existence had been spent in the narrow, dark office, which was still decorated with the

same wall paper. He had entered there as a young
man, as assistant to Monsieur Brument, and with
the desire to replace him.

He had taken his place and wished for nothing
more.

The whole harvest of memories which other men
reap in their span of years, the unexpected events,
sweet or tragic loves, adventurous journeys, all the
occurrences of a free existence, all these things had
remained unknown to him.

Days, weeks, months, seasons, years, all were
alike to him. He got up every day at the same
hour, started out, arrived at the office, ate luncheon,
went away, had dinner, and went to bed without
ever interrupting the regular monotony of similar
actions, deeds, and thoughts.

Formerly he used to look at his blond mustache
and wavy hair in the little round mirror left by
his predecessor. Now, every evening before leaving,
he would look at his white mustache and bald head
in the same mirror. Forty years had rolled by,
long and rapid, dreary as a day of sadness and as
similar as the hours of a nightmare! Forty years
of which nothing remained, not even a memory, not
even a misfortune, since the death of his parents.
Nothing.

That day Monsieur Leras stood by the door,
dazzled at the brilliancy of the setting sun; and instead of returning home he decided to take a little
stroll before dinner, a thing which happened to him
four or five times a year.

He reached the boulevards, where people were
streaming along under the green trees. It was a
spring evening, one of those first warm and pleasant
evenings which fill the heart with the joy of life.

Monsieur Leras went along with his mincing old man's step; he was going along with joy in his heart, at peace with the world. He reached the Champs-Elysées, and he continued to walk, enlivened at the sight of the young people trotting along.

The whole sky was aflame; the Arc de Triomphe stood out against the brilliant background of the horizon, like a giant surrounded by fire. As he approached the gigantic monument, the old bookkeeper noticed that he was hungry, and he went into a wine dealer's for dinner.

The meal was served in front of the store, on the sidewalk; it consisted of some mutton, salad, and asparagus; it was the best dinner that Monsieur Leras had had in a long time. He washed down his cheese with a small bottle of burgundy, had his after-dinner cup of coffee, a thing which he rarely took, and finally a little pony of brandy.

When he had paid he felt quite youthful, even a little moved. And he said to himself: "What a fine evening! I will continue my stroll as far as the entrance to the Bois de Boulogne. It will do me good."

He set out. An old tune which one of his neighbors used to sing kept returning to his mind. He kept on humming it over and over again. A hot, still night had fallen over Paris. Monsieur Leras was following along the Avenue du Bois de Boulogne and watching the cabs drive by. They kept coming with their shining lights, one behind the other, giving him a glimpse of the couples inside, the women in their light dresses and the men dressed in black.

It was one long procession of lovers, riding under the warm, starlit sky. They kept on coming in rapid succession. They passed by in the carriages, pressed against each other, lost in their dreams, in the emotion of desire, in the anticipation of the approaching embrace. The warm shadows seemed to be full of floating kisses. A sensation of tenderness filled the air. All these embracing couples, all these people intoxicated with the same idea, with the same thought, made the atmosphere around them feverish.

At last Monsieur Leras grew a little tired of walking, and he sat down on a bench to watch these carriages pass by with their burdens of love. Almost immediately a woman walked up to him and said: " Good evening, papa."

He did not answer, and she continued: " Let me love you, dearie; you'll see how nice I can be."

He answered: " Madame, you are mistaken."

She slipped her arm through his, saying: " Come along, now; don't be foolish, listen. . . ."

He arose and walked away, with sadness in his heart. A few yards away another woman walked up to him and asked: " Won't you sit down beside me? "

He said: " What makes you do that? "

She stood before him and in an altered, hoarse, angry voice exclaimed: " Well, it isn't for the fun of it, anyhow! "

He insisted in a gentle voice: " Then what makes you? "

She grumbled: " I've got to live! Foolish question! " And she walked away, humming.

Monsieur Leras stood there bewildered. Other women were passing near him, speaking to him and calling to him. He felt as though he were enveloped in darkness, by something disagreeable.

He sat down again on a bench; the carriages were still rolling by. He thought: " I should have done better not to come here; I feel all upset."

He began to think of all this venal or passionate love, of all these kisses, sold or given, which were passing by in front of him. Love! He scarcely knew it. In his lifetime he had only known two or three women, his means forcing him to live a quiet life, and he looked back at the life which he had led, so different from everybody else, so dreary, so mournful, so empty.

Some people are really unfortunate. And sud-denly, as though a veil had been torn from his eyes, he perceived the infinite misery, the monotony of his existence: the past, present, and future misery; his last day similar to his first one, with nothing before him, behind him or about him, nothing in his heart or any place.

The stream of carriages was still going by. In the rapid passage of the open cab he still saw the two silent and embracing creatures. It seemed to him that the whole of humanity was flowing on before him, intoxicated with joy, pleasure, and happiness. He alone was looking on. To-morrow he would again be alone, always alone, more so than any one else. He stood up, took a few steps, and suddenly he felt as tired as though he had taken a long journey on foot, and he sat down on the next bench.

What was he waiting for? What was he hoping for? Nothing. He was thinking of how pleasant it must be in old age to return home and find the little children. It is pleasant to grow old when one is surrounded by those beings who owe their life to you, who love you, who caress you, who tell you charming and foolish little things which warm your heart and console you for everything.

And, thinking of his empty room, clean and sad, where no one but himself ever entered, a feeling of distress filled his soul; and the place seemed to him more mournful even than his little office. Nobody ever came there; no one ever spoke in it. It was dead, silent, without the echo of a human voice. It seems as though the walls retain something of the people who live within them, something of their manner, face and voice. The houses inhabited by happy families are gayer than the dwellings of the unfortunate. His room was as barren of memories as his life. And the thought of returning to this place, all alone, of getting into his bed, of doing over again all the movements and actions of every evening, this thought terrified him. As though to escape farther from this sinister home, and from the time when he would have to return to it, he arose and walked out on the grass behind the bushes.

About him, above him, everywhere, he heard the continuous, immense, confused rumble, composed of countless and different noises, a vague and great palpitation of life: the breath of Paris, breathing like a giant.

The sun was already shedding a flood of light on the Bois de Boulogne. Several carriages were beginning to drive about, and people were appearing on horseback.

A couple was walking through a deserted alley. Suddenly the young woman raised her eyes and saw something brown in the branches. Surprised and anxious, she raised her hand, exclaiming: "Look! what is that?"

Then she shrieked and fell into the arms of her

companion, who was forced to place her on the ground.

The policeman who had been called took down an old man who had hung himself with his suspenders.

Examination showed that he had died on the evening before. The papers found on him showed that he was a bookkeeper with Messieurs Labuze and Company, and that his name was Leras.

The death was attributed to suicide, the cause of which could not be suspected. Perhaps a sudden access of madness!

# The Door

H!" exclaimed Karl Massouligny, "the question of complaisant husbands is a difficult one. I have seen many kinds, and yet I am unable to give an opinion about any of them. I have often tried to determine whether they are blind, weak, or clairvoyant. I believe that there are some which belong to each of these categories that I have mentioned.

"Let us quickly pass over the blind ones. They cannot rightly be called complaisant, since they do not know, but they are good creatures who cannot see farther than their nose. It is a curious and interesting thing to notice the ease with which men and women can be deceived. We are taken in by the slightest trick of those who surround us. Of our children, our friends, our servants, our tradespeople. Humanity is credulous, and in order to discover deceit of others, we do not display one-

tenth the finesse which we use when we, in turn,
wish to deceive some one else.

" The clairvoyant husbands can be divided into
three classes. Those who have some interest, pe-
cuniary, ambitious or otherwise, in their wife's having a lover, or lovers. These ask only to safe-
guard appearances as near as possible, and they are
satisfied.

" Next come those who get angry. What a beautiful novel one could write about them!

" Finally the weak ones! Those who are afraid
of scandal.

" There are also those who are powerless, or,
rather, tired, who escape the conjugal bed from fear
of ataxia or apoplexy, who are satisfied to see a
friend run these risks.

" But I have met a husband of a rare species,
and who guarded against the common accident in a
strange and witty manner.

" In Paris I had made the acquaintance of an
elegant, fashionable couple. The woman, nervous,
tall, slender, courted, was supposed to have had
many adventures. She pleased me with her wit,
and I believe that I pleased her, also. I courted her,
a trial courting to which she answered with evident
provocations. Soon we arrived at the edge of tender
glances, pressures of the hands, all the little gallantries which precede the great attack.

" Nevertheless, I hesitated. I believe that, as
a rule, the majority of society intrigues, however
short they may be, are not worth the trouble which
they give us and the difficulties which may arise. I
therefore mentally compared the advantages and
disadvantages which I could expect, and I thought
that the husband suspected me.

" One evening, at a ball, as I was saying tender things to the young woman in a little parlor leading from the big hall where the dancing was going on, I noticed in a mirror the reflection of some one who was watching us. It was he. Our looks met and then I saw him turn his head and walk away.

" I murmured: ' Your husband is spying on us.'

" She seemed dumfounded, and asked: ' My husband? '

" ' Yes, he has been watching us for some time.'

" ' Nonsense! Are you sure? '

" ' Very sure.'

" ' How strange! He is usually very pleasant with all my friends.'

" ' Perhaps he guessed that I love you! '

" ' Nonsense! You were not the first one to pay attention to me. Every woman who is a little in view drags behind her a herd of sighers.'

" ' Yes. But I love you deeply.'

" ' Admitting that that is true, does a husband ever guess those things? '

" ' Then he is not jealous? '

" ' No—no! '

" She thought for an instant, and then continued: ' No. I do not think that I ever noticed any jealousy on his part.'

" ' Has he never—watched you? '

" ' No. As I said, he is always agreeable to my friends.'

" From that day my courting became much more assiduous. The woman did not please me any more than before, but the probable jealousy of her husband tempted me greatly.

" As for her, I judged her coolly and clearly.

She had a certain worldly charm, due to a quick, gay, amiable, and superficial mind, but no real, deep attraction. She was, as I have already said, a little nervous, and quite elegant. How can I explain myself? It was . . . a decoration, not a home.

" One day, after taking dinner with her, her husband said to me, just as I was leaving: ' My dear friend' (he now called me ' friend '), ' we soon

leave for the country. It is a great pleasure for my wife and myself to receive the people whom we like. We would like to have you spend a month with us. It would be very nice of you to do so.'

" I was dumfounded, but I accepted.

" A month later I arrived at their estate of Vertcresson, in Touraine. They were waiting for me at the station, five miles from the château. There were three of them, she, the husband, and a gentleman unknown to me, the Comte de Morterade, to whom I was introduced. He appeared to be delighted to make my acquaintance, and the strangest ideas passed through my mind while we trotted along the beautiful road between two hedges. I was saying to myself: ' Let's see, what can this mean? Here is a husband who cannot doubt that his wife and I are on more than friendly terms, and yet he invites me to his house, receives me like an old friend, and seems to say: '' Go ahead, my friend, the road is clear! ''

'' ' Then I am introduced to a very pleasant gentleman, who seems already to have settled down in the house, and . . . and who is perhaps trying to get out of it, and who seems as pleased at my arrival as the husband himself.

'' ' Is it some former lover who wishes to retire? One might think so. But, then, would these two men tacitly have come to one of these infamous little agreements so common in society? And it is proposed to me that I should quietly enter into the association and take up the continuation of it. All hands and arms are held out to me. All doors and hearts are open to me.

'' ' And what about her? An enigma. She cannot be ignorant of everything. However? . . . however? . . . that's it. I understand nothing.'

'' The dinner was very gay and cordial. On leaving the table the husband and his friend began to play cards, while I went out on the porch to look at the moonlight with Madame. She seemed to be greatly moved by nature, and I judged that the moment for my happiness was near. That evening she was really delightful. The country had seemed to make her more tender. Her long slender waist looked pretty on this stone porch beside a great vase in which grew some flowers. I felt like dragging her out under the trees, throwing myself at her feet, and speaking to her words of love.

'' Her husband's voice called: ' Louise? '

'' ' Yes, my dear.'

'' ' You are forgetting the tea.'

'' ' I will have it brought, my friend.'

" We returned to the house, and she served us
with tea. When the two men had finished playing
cards, they were visibly tired. I had to go to my
room. I did not get to sleep till late, and then I
slept badly.

" An excursion was decided upon for the following afternoon, and we went in an open carriage to
visit some ruins. She and I were in the back of the
vehicle and they were opposite us, riding back-
ward. The conversation was sympathetic and agreeable. I am an orphan, and it seemed to me as
though I had just found my family, I felt so at home
with them.

" Suddenly, as she had stretched out her foot
between her husband's feet, he murmured reproach-
fully: ' Louise, please don't use up your old shoes
yourself. There is no reason for being neater in
Paris than in the country.'

" I lowered my eyes. She was indeed wearing
worn-out shoes, and I noticed that her stockings
were not pulled up tightly.

" She had blushed and hidden her foot under
her dress. The friend was looking out in the distance, with an indifferent and unconcerned look.

" The husband offered me a cigar, which I accepted. For a few days it was impossible for me to
be alone with her for two minutes; he was with us
everywhere. He was delightful to me.

" One morning he came to get me to take a walk
before breakfast, and the conversation happened to
turn to marriage. I spoke a little about solitude,
and about how charming life can be made by a
woman. Suddenly he interrupted me, saying: ' My
friend, don't talk about things you know nothing
about. A woman who has no more reason for lov-

ing you will not love you for a long time. All the
little coquetries which make them so exquisite
when they do not definitely belong to us cease as
soon as they become ours. And then . . . the
respectable women . . . that is to say, our wives
. . . are . . . are not . . . quite . . .
do not understand their profession of wife. Do you
understand? '

" He said no more, and I could not guess his
thoughts.

" Two days after this conversation he called me
to his room quite early in order to show me a collection of engravings. I sat in an easy-chair opposite the big door which separated his apartment
from his wife's, and behind this door I heard some
one walking and moving, and I was thinking very
little of the engravings, although I kept exclaiming:
' Oh, charming! delightful! exquisite! '

" He suddenly said: ' Oh! I have a beautiful
specimen in the next room. I'll go get it.'

" He ran to the door quickly, and both sides
opened as though for a theatrical effect.

" In a large room, all in disorder, in the midst
of skirts, collars, waists lying around on the floor,
stood a tall, dried-up creature. The lower part of
her body was covered with an old, worn-out silk petticoat, which was hanging limply on her shapeless
form, and she was standing in front of a mirror
brushing some short, sparse blond hairs. Her arms
formed two acute angles, and as she turned around
in astonishment I saw under a common cotton
chemise a regular cemetery of ribs, usually hidden from the public gaze by well-arranged pads.

" The husband uttered a natural cry and came
back, closing the doors, and said: ' Gracious! how

stupid I am! Oh, how thoughtless! My wife will never forgive me for that!'

"I already felt like thanking him. I left three days later, after cordially shaking hands with the two men and kissing the lady's fingers; she bade me a cold good-by."

Karl Massouligny was silent. Some one asked: "But what was the friend?"

"I don't know . . . however . . . however, he looked greatly distressed to see me leaving so soon."

# The Night of the Wedding

OR a long time Jacques Bourdil-lère had sworn that he would never marry; but he suddenly changed his mind. It happened suddenly, one summer, at the sea-shore.

One morning, as he lay stretched out on the sand, watching the women coming out of the water, a little foot had struck him by its neatness and daintiness. He looked up higher and was delighted with the whole person. By the way, he could see nothing but the ankles and the head emerging from a flannel bathrobe carefully held closed. He was supposed to be sensual and a fast liver. It was, therefore, only through the grace-ful form that he was at first captured; then he was held by the charm of the young girl's sweet mind, so simple and good, as fresh as her cheeks and lips.

He was presented to the family and pleased them; he immediately fell madly in love. When he would see Berthe Lannis in the distance, on the long yellow stretch of sand, he would tingle to the roots of his hair. When he was near her he would become silent, unable to speak or even to think, with a kind of bubbling in his heart, of buzzing in his ears, and of bewilderment in his mind. Was that love?

He did not know or understand, but he had fully decided to have this child for his wife.

Her parents hesitated for a long time, restrained by the young man's bad reputation. It was said that he had an old sweetheart, one of these binding attachments which one always believes to be broken off and yet which always hold.

Besides, for a shorter or longer period, he loved every woman who came within reach of his lips.

Then he settled down and refused, even once, to see the one with whom he had lived for so long. A friend took care of this woman's pension and assured her an income. Jacques paid, but he did not even wish to hear of her, pretending even to ignore her name. She wrote him letters which he never opened. Every week he would recognize the clumsy writing of the abandoned woman, and every week a greater anger surged within him against her, and he would quickly tear the envelope and the paper, without opening it, without reading one single line, knowing in advance the reproaches and complaints which it contained.

As but little faith existed in his constancy, the test was prolonged through the winter, and Berthe's hand was not granted him until the spring. The wedding took place in Paris at the beginning of May.

The young couple had decided not to take the conventional wedding trip; but after a little dance

for the younger cousins, which would not be prolonged after eleven o'clock in order that this day of
lengthy ceremonies might not be too tiresome, the
young pair were to spend the first night in the pa-
rental home and then, on the following morning, to
leave for the beach so dear to their hearts where
they had known and loved each other.

Night had come, and the dance was going on in
the large parlor. The two had retired to a little
Japanese boudoir, hung with bright silks and dimly
lighted by the soft rays of a large colored lantern
hanging from the ceiling like a gigantic egg.
Through the open window the fresh air from outside passed over their faces like a caress, for the
night was warm and calm, full of the odor of spring.

They were saying nothing to each other; they
were holding each other's hands, and from time to
time squeezing them with all their might. She sat
there with a dreamy look, feeling a little lost by this
great change in her life, but smiling, moved, ready
to cry, often, also, ready almost to faint from joy,
believing the whole world to be changed by what had
just happened to her, nervous she knew not why,
and feeling her whole body and soul filled by an in-
definable and delicious lassitude.

He was looking at her persistently with a fixed
smile. He wished to speak, but found nothing to
say, and so sat there, putting all his ardor in pressures of the hand. From time to time he would
murmur: " Berthe! " And each time she would
raise her eyes to him with a look of tenderness; they
would look at each other for a second, and then her
look, pierced and fascinated by his, would fall.

They found no thoughts to exchange. They had
been left alone, but occasionally some of the dancers

would cast a rapid glance at them, as though they were the discreet and trusting witnesses of a mystery.

A door opened and a servant entered, holding on a tray a letter which a messenger had just brought. Jacques, trembling, took this paper, overwhelmed by a vague and sudden fear, the mysterious terror of swift misfortune.

He looked for a long time at the envelope, the writing on which he did not know, not daring to open it, not wishing to read it, with a wild desire to put it in his pocket and say to himself: " I'll leave that till to-morrow, when I'm far away! " But on one corner two words stared at him: " *Very urgent,*" filling him with terror. Saying: " Please excuse me, my dear," he tore open the envelope. He read the paper, grew frightfully pale, looked over it again, and, slowly, he seemed to spell it out word for word.

When he raised his head his whole face was upset. He stammered: " My dear, it . . . it's from my best friend, who has had a very great misfortune. He has need of me immediately . . . for a matter of life or death. Will you excuse me if I leave you for half an hour? I'll be right back."

Trembling and dazed, she stammered: " Go then, my dear! " not yet having been his wife long enough to dare to question him, to demand to know. He disappeared. She remained alone, listening to the dancing in the neighboring parlor.

He had seized up the first hat and coat he came to and jumped down the stairs three at a time. As he was emerging into the street he stopped under the gas-jet of the vestibule and re-read the letter. This is what it said:

" SIR: A girl by the name of Ravet, an old sweetheart of
yours, it seems, has just given birth to a child whom she
claims to be yours.  The mother is about to die and is begging for you.  I take the liberty to write and ask you if you
can grant this last request to a woman who seems to be very
unhappy and worthy of pity.          Yours truly,

" DR. BONNARD."

When he reached the sick-room the woman was
already on the point of death.  He did not recognize her at first.  The doctor and two nurses were
taking care of her.  And everywhere on the floor
were pails full of ice and rags covered with blood.
Water flooded the carpet; two candles were burning
on a bureau; behind the bed, in a little wicker crib,
the child was crying, and each time it would moan
the mother, in torture, would try to move, shivering
under her ice bandages.

She was wounded to death by this birth.  Her
life was flowing from her; and, notwithstanding the
ice and the care, the merciless hemorrhage continued, hastening her last hour.

She recognized Jacques, and wished to raise her
arms.  They were so weak that she could not, but
down her pallid cheeks coursed tears.

He dropped to his knees beside the bed, seized
one of her hands, and kissed it frantically; then, little by little, he drew nearer to the thin face, which
started at the contact.  One of the nurses was light-
ing them with a candle, and the doctor was watching them from the back of the room.

Then she said, in a voice which sounded as
though it came from a distance: " I am going to
die, dear; promise to stay to the end.  Oh! don't
leave me now.  Don't leave me at the last minute! "

He kissed her face and her hair, and, weeping, he murmured: " Never fear, I will stay."

It was several minutes before she could speak again, she was so weak. She continued: " The little one is yours. I swear it before God and on my soul. I swear it as I am dying! I have never loved another man but you—promise to take care of the child."

He was trying to take this poor pain-racked body in his arms. Maddened by remorse and sorrow, he stammered: " I swear to you that I will bring him up and love him. He shall never leave me."

Then she tried to kiss Jacques. Powerless to lift her head, she held out her white lips in an appeal for a kiss. He approached his lips to pluck this poor caress.

As soon as she felt a little calmer, she murmured: " Bring him here, and let me see if you love him."

He went and got the child. He placed him gently on the bed between them, and the little one stopped crying. She murmured: " Don't move any more!" And he was quiet. And he stayed there, holding in his burning hand this other one shaken by the shivers of death, just as, a while ago, he had been holding a hand trembling with love. From time to time he would cast a quick glance at the clock, which marked midnight, then one o'clock, then two.

The physician had returned; the two nurses, after noiselessly moving around through the room for a while, were now sleeping on chairs. The child was sleeping, and the mother, with eyes shut, appeared also to be resting.

Suddenly, just as pale daylight was creeping in behind the curtains, she stretched out her arms with such a quick and violent motion that she almost threw her baby on the floor. A kind of rattle was heard in her throat, then she lay on her back motionless, dead.

The nurses sprang forward and declared: "All is over!"

He looked once more at this woman whom he had so loved, then at the clock, which pointed to four, and he ran away, forgetting his overcoat, in evening dress, with the child in his arms.

After she had been left alone, the young wife had waited, calmly enough at first, in the little Japanese boudoir. Then, as she did not see him return, she went back to the parlor with an indifferent and calm appearance, but terribly anxious. When her mother saw her alone she asked: "Where is your husband?" She answered: "In his room; he is coming back soon."

After an hour, when everybody had questioned her, she told about the letter, Jacques's upset appearance, and her fears of an accident.

Still they waited. The guests left; only the nearest relatives remained. At midnight the bride was put to bed, all shaken by tears. Her mother and two aunts, sitting around the bed, were listening to her cry, silent and in despair . . . the father had gone to the commissary of police to see if he could obtain some news.

At five o'clock a slight noise was heard in the hall; a door was softly opened and closed; then suddenly a little cry like the mewing of a cat was heard throughout the silent house.

All the women started forward, and Berthe

sprang ahead of them all, pushing her way past her aunts, wrapped in a bathrobe.

Jacques stood in the middle of the room, pale and panting, holding an infant in his arms. The four women looked at him, astonished; but Berthe, who had suddenly become courageous, rushed forward with anguish in her heart, exclaiming: " What is it? What's the matter? "

He looked around wildly and answered shortly: " I—I have a child, and the mother has just died. . . ." And in his clumsy hands he held out the howling infant.

Without saying a word, Berthe seized the child, kissed it, and hugged it to her; then she raised her tear-filled eyes to him, asking: " Did you say that the mother was dead? " He answered: " Yes—in my arms . . . I had broken with her since summer . . . I knew nothing. The physician sent for me."

Then Berthe murmured: " Well, we will bring up the little one."

# The Revenge

HE little Baroness de la Grangerie was slumbering on her sofa when the little Marquise de Rennedou entered quickly, with an excited appearance, her waist a little rumpled, her hat slightly awry, and she fell into a chair, exclaiming: " Oof! That's over! "

Her friend, who knew her to be ordinarily calm and gentle, sat up in surprise, and asked: " What? What have you done? "

The Marquise, who seemed to be unable to stay in one place, stood up and began to walk around the room, then she threw herself down at the foot of the sofa where her friend was resting and took her hands, saying: " Listen, dear; swear to me never to repeat what I shall tell you! "

" I swear."

" On all that you hold holy! "

" On all that I hold holy."

" Well, I have just taken vengeance on Simon."

The other exclaimed: " Oh! you certainly did well."

" Didn't I, though? Why, for the last six months he has been even more unbearable than formerly. When I married him I knew that he was homely, but I thought that he was kind. How mistaken I was! He undoubtedly thought that I loved him for himself, with his big stomach and his red nose, for he began to coo like a turtle-dove. As you can imagine, it made me laugh; from that time I called him ' Pigeon.'

" Really, men have funny ideas about themselves. When he understood that the only sentiment which I had for him was friendliness, he became suspicious, he began to say mean things about me, to call me a coquette, a sly person, I know not what. And then things became worse after . . . after . . . it's very hard to explain what I mean. . . . Well, he was very much in love with me . . . very much so . . . and he proved it to me often . . . too often. Oh! my dear, what torture to be . . . loved by a grotesque man. . . . No, really, I couldn't any longer . . . it was like having a tooth pulled out every evening . . . even worse; just imagine some one of your acquaintance who is very ugly, very ridiculous, very repulsive, with an enormous stomach . . . that's the worst part of it . . . and big, fat, hairy legs. You see what I mean, don't you? Well, just imagine that that person is your husband . . . and that . . . you understand. Oh! It's odious! Perfectly odious! . . . Positively, it—it made me ill—it actually gave me nausea. Really, this couldn't go on any longer. There ought to be some law to protect women in such a case.

" It's not because I have dreamed of poetic love; no, I never did that. It is no longer to be found. All the men nowadays are grooms or bankers; they only love either horses or money, and if they love women it's the same way that they love horses; it is to show them off in their homes, just as they parade a beautiful pair of roans. Nothing more. Life is such to-day that sentiment can have no part in it.

" Let us, therefore, live like practical and indifferent women. Interrelations are no longer anything but regular meetings where each time the same things are said. For whom could we have a little affection and tenderness? The men, our men, are usually nothing more than very correct puppets who completely lack all intelligence and delicacy. If we look for a little wit, as one looks for water in the desert, we draw to us all the artists, and then we are surrounded by unbearable posers or ill-bred bohemians. Like Diogenes, I am looking for a man in the whole of Parisian society; but I am already quite sure that I will not find him, and it will not be long before I blow out my lantern. To return to my husband; as it thoroughly upset me to see him enter my room in his bare legs, I employed every means, every possible means, to keep him away and to—to disgust him with me. At first he was furious; then he became jealous; he imagined that I was deceiving him. In the beginning he was satisfied with watching me. He would watch every motion of any man who entered the house; then the persecution began. He followed me everywhere. He employed the most abominable means to surprise me. After that he allowed me to speak with no one.

At a ball he would stand behind me, pushing forward his thick dog's face as soon as I would say a word. He would follow me to the buffet, forbidding me to dance with this one or with that one, or else he would take me away in the middle of a cotillon, making me appear stupid and ridiculous. Then I ceased to go into society.

" In intimate life it became even worse. Just imagine, one day he called me . . . I don't dare say the word, my dear! . . . In the evening he would say to me: ' Well, who was your lover to-day? ' I would cry, and he would be delighted.

" It became even worse than that. Last week he took me to dinner on the Champs Elysées. Fate willed that Baubignac should be sitting at the next table. Then Simon began to crush my feet under the table, and to grunt at me: ' You had an engagement with him; just wait till I get hold of you! ' Then, my dear, you can never imagine what he did: he gently drew my hat-pin out and stuck it into my arm. I uttered a shriek. Everybody crowded around us. Then he pretended to be sorry. You understand. Then I decided that I would avenge myself immediately. What would you have done in my place? "

" Why, I should have taken the same position! "

" Well, it's done."

" How? "

" What? Don't you understand? "

" But, my dear . . ."

" Well, yes . . ."

" Yes, what? "

" Just imagine his expression. Can't you see him with his heavy face, his red nose, and his side whiskers, which hang like a dog's ears? "

" Yes."

" And then, think he is as jealous as a cat! "

" Yes."

" Well, I said to myself: ' I'm going to get revenge for myself and for Marie,' for I fully expected to tell you, but only you. Just imagine his expression, and then think that he . . . he . . . he is . . ."

" What . . . you . . . ? "

"But, my dear, for goodness' sake, swear that you never will tell any one! But isn't it funny? . . . Why, from that time he seems to be entirely different! And I can't help laughing . . . all by myself . . . just think of him! "

The Baroness was looking at her friend, and she began to laugh wildly, hysterically, with her hands on her dress, her breath coming short, and leaning forward as if she would fall on her face.

Then the little Marquise also burst out in laughter, and she kept repeating: " Think . . . think of it . . . isn't it funny? . . . Can't you . . . can't you see him? . . . Think of his whiskers! . . . His nose! . . . Isn't it funny? . . . But . . . promise . . . promise never to tell! "

They were almost choking, unable to speak, crying real tears in this delirium of gayety. The Baroness was the first to calm down; and still out of breath, she asked: " Oh! Tell me how it happened . . . tell me . . . it's so . . . so funny! . . ."

But the other one was unable to speak; she kept stammering: " When I had taken my decision . . . I said to myself . . . ' Quickly . . . quickly . . . it must happen right away! ' . . . And I . . . I did it to-day . . ."

" To-day! . . ."

" Yes . . . just a while ago . . . and I told Simon to meet me here so that we could have some fun. . . . He is coming . . . shortly! He is coming! . . . Just . . . just . . . just think of it when you look at him! "

The Baroness was panting as if she had been running a race. She continued: " Oh! tell me how you managed it . . . tell me! . . ."

" It's very simple. . . . I said to myself: ' He is jealous of Baubignac; well, Baubignac it shall be. He is as thick as a stone wall, but very honest. He would be incapable of telling anybody.' Then I went to his house after lunch."

" You went to see him? On what pretext? "

" A subscription . . . for the orphans . . ."

" Tell me . . . quick . . . tell me about it . . ."

" He was so surprised at seeing me that he was unable to speak. And then he gave me two louis for my subscription; and then, as I was rising to leave, he asked about my husband; then I pretended to be unable to contain myself any longer, and I told him everything that was on my mind. I even made him out worse than he is! . . . Then Baubignac grew sorry for me, he tried to find some way of helping me . . . and I began to cry . . . as if my heart were broken . . . he tried to comfort me . . . and when I did not grow any calmer, he kissed me . . . I kept repeating: ' Oh! my poor friend! . . . My poor friend! ' He kept repeating, ' My poor friend! . . . my poor friend! ' . . . And all the time he kept kissing me; and . . . and . . . there!

" After that I grew angry and heaped re-

proaches on him. Oh! I treated him as though he
were the last of the last . . . but I felt a mad
desire to laugh. I kept thinking of Simon and his
whiskers! Just imagine . . . ! Just imagine!
I simply couldn't keep my face straight as I was
coming here. Just think of it! . . . It's done!
. . . Whatever may happen now, it's done! And
he was so afraid of that very thing! There may be
wars, earthquakes, epidemics, we may all die . . .
it's done! Nothing can help that! Think of it when
you look at him! ''

The Baroness, who was choking, asked: '' Do
you intend to see Baubignac again? ''

'' No, indeed! . . . I've had enough of him
. . . he would be no better than my husband! ''

And both of them began to laugh madly again.
The tinkle of a bell interrupted their laughter.

The Marquise murmured: '' It's he . . . look
at him! ''

The door opened. And a fat, red-faced man,
with thick lips and hanging whiskers, appeared. He
was rolling angry eyes.

The two young women looked at him for a minute, and then they threw themselves down upon the
sofa, shaken by a fit of violent laughter.

And he kept repeating angrily: '' What's the
matter? Are you mad? . . . Are you mad? . . .
Are you mad? ''

# The Woodcocks

Y dear, you ask me why I do
not return to Paris; you are
surprised and almost angry.
The reason which I will give
you will probably shock
you; does a hunter go to
Paris during the season of
the woodcocks?

Certainly, I like this city
life which extends from the
chamber to the sidewalk, but
I prefer the free, rough autumn life of the hunter.

In Paris it seems to me as if I were never out
of doors; for the streets are really nothing more
than great apartments without ceilings. You are
not outside when you are between two walls, your
feet on the stone or wooden pavement, your view
barred everywhere by buildings, without any horizon of pastures, plains, or forests. Thousands of
neighbors elbow and push about, bow and speak;
and the fact that I get water on my umbrella when
it is raining is not sufficient to give me the impression, the sensation of space.

Here I perceive clearly and delightfully the difference between inside and outside . . . but it is not of that that I wish to speak to you. . . .

The woodcocks are here.

I must tell you that I live in a great country house in Normandy, in a valley near a small river, and that I am hunting almost every day.

On other days I read; even things which men in Paris have no time to know, serious, deep, curious things written by a genius, a stranger who has spent his whole life studying the same question, and who has observed facts relative to the influence of the function of our organs on our intelligence.

But I want to tell you of the woodcocks. My two friends, the D'Orgemol brothers, and myself are remaining here throughout the hunting season, waiting for the first cold weather. As soon as there is a frost, we leave for their farm at Cannetot, near Fécamp, because there is there a delightful little forest where dwell all the passing woodcocks.

You know the D'Orgemols, these two giants of early Normandy, these two men of the ancient, conquering race which invaded France, took and kept England, settled along every coast of the old world, built cities everywhere, swept over Sicily and created an admirable art there, defeated all the kings, pillaged all the proud cities, overthrew and outwitted popes, and especially left children in every bed on the earth. The D'Orgemols are two typical Normans; everything about them flavors of Normandy, the voice, the accent, the wit, the blond hair, and the eyes, color of the sea.

When we are together we speak in dialect, we live, think, act like Normans, we become more Norman than our farmers themselves.

Well, we have been expecting the woodcocks for
the last two weeks. Every morning the elder brother, Simon, would say to me: " Well, the wind is
turning to the east; there is going to be a frost;
they'll be here in a couple of days."

The younger brother, Gaspard, more precise,
would wait until the frost was there before announc-
ing it.

Last Thursday he came into my room at daybreak, and cried: " It's here! The whole ground
is white. Two more days like this and we'll leave
for Cannetot."

And, in fact, two days later we were leaving for
Cannetot. You certainly would have laughed if you
could have seen us. We were traveling in a strange
hunting wagon which my father had formerly con-
structed. " Construct " is the only word which I
can use when speaking of this monumental traveler,
or, rather, of this rolling earthquake. It contains
everything: boxes for provisions, boxes for weap-
ons, for trunks, for everything that is necessary.
Everything is under cover except the men, who have
to sit on benches as high as a third-story window,
and supported by four gigantic wheels. One gets
up there as best one can, making use of the feet,
hands, and even the teeth, for no step gives access
to this edifice.

The two D'Orgemols and myself scramble up on
this mountain, dressed like Laplanders. We are
wearing sheepskins, thick woolen stockings over our
trousers, and gaiters over our stockings; besides
this, we wear black fur hats and white fur gloves.
When we are settled, Jean, my servant, throws up
our three dogs, Pif, Paf, and Mustache. Pif belongs
to Simon, Paf to Gaspard, and Mustache to me.

They look like three hairy little crocodiles. They are long, close to the earth, with crooked legs and very hairy. One can hardly see their black eyes under the hair, and their white fangs under their beards. We never shut them up in the rolling kennels of the wagon. We make our dogs lie at our feet, in order to keep ourselves warm. We leave, and get abominably shaken up. The weather was freezing. We were pleased. We arrived at about five. The farmer, Maître Picot, was waiting before the door. He is a strapping fellow, not tall, but short and stocky, as vigorous as a bulldog, as sly as a fox, always smiling, always happy and making money out of everything.

The woodcock season is a great time for him. The farmhouse is a big rambling building, with a yard full of apple trees, and surrounded by four hedges. We go into the kitchen, where a big fire is burning in honor of our arrival.

The table is set near the high fireplace, where everything is cooking; in front of the bright flame is a plump chicken, the gravy from which is dripping into an earthen vessel.

The farmer's wife comes up and treats us. She is a big, silent, very polite woman, always busy with her housekeeping, her head full of business and figures, the price of grain, of poultry, sheep, cattle. She is an orderly and severe woman, known throughout the neighborhood.

In the back of the kitchen is the big table where shortly the servants of every description, truck drivers, laborers, farm girls, shepherds, will sit down; and all these people will eat in silence under the active eye of the mistress, and watch us dine with Maître Picot, who will tell us jokes. Then, when the employees shall have eaten, Madame Picot will take her frugal meal alone, on a corner of the table, while she watches the maid. On ordinary days she eats with the others.

The D'Orgemols and myself, all three of us, sleep in a large, bare whitewashed room which contains only our three beds, three chairs, and three wash-basins. Gaspard always wakes first, and he rouses the rest of us. In a half hour everybody is ready, and we leave with Maître Picot, who hunts with us.

Maître Picot prefers me to his masters. Why? Doubtless because I am not his master. The two of us reach the woods from the right-hand side, while the two brothers attack it from the left. Simon takes care of the dogs, which he drags along, all three on one leash. For we are not hunting woodcock, but rabbits. We are convinced that one should not hunt woodcock, but find it. You run across it and kill it, that's all. If you try to look for it you will never find it. It is really a beautiful and curious thing to hear, in the fresh morning air, the sharp explosion of the guns, and then Gaspard's stentorian voice fill the air and cry: '' Woodcock! ''

I am sly. When I have killed a woodcock, I cry: '' Rabbit! '' And my triumph is double when the game is taken from the bags at noon.

Well, Maître Picot and I are in the little forest, where the leaves are falling with a soft and continuous rustle, a sad, dry noise; they are dead. It is cold, a cold which stings the eyes, the nose and the ears, and which has powdered the grass and the brown ground with a white powder. But under the long sheepskins we feel warm. The sun looks gay in the blue sky; it scarcely warms at all, but it is gay. How delightful it is to hunt through the woods on a fresh winter's morning!

A dog barks sharply. It is Pif. I know his voice. Then nothing more. I hear a cry, then another; than Paf in turn makes himself heard. What can Mustache be doing? Ah! there he is, clucking like a strangled chicken. They have found a rabbit. They go away, draw nearer, go off again, then return; we follow their unexpected tracks, running along the little paths, our minds alert and our fingers on the trigger.

They go out toward the fields, we follow them. Suddenly a gray shadow crosses the path. I throw my gun to my shoulder and shoot. The light smoke clears off in the blue air, and I see a bundle of white hair kicking about on the grass. Then I bawl at the top of my lungs: "Rabbit! rabbit!" Then I show it to the three dogs, to the three hairy crocodiles, who congratulate me by wagging their tails; then they go to look for another.

Maître Picot had joined me. Mustache began to bark. The farmer said: "It might be a hare; let us go to the edge of the field."

But just as I was leaving the woods I saw, standing right near me, Maître Picot's dumb shepherd, Gargan; he was wrapped in an immense yellow cloak, his head was covered by a woolen bonnet, and he was knitting a stocking. According to the custom, I said: "Good morning, pastor." He raised his hand to greet me, although he had not heard my voice; but he had seen the movement of my lips. I had known this shepherd for fifteen years. For fifteen years I had seen him every autumn standing in the middle or at the edge of a field, his body motionless, and his hands always knitting. His herd followed him leisurely and seemed to obey his very glances.

Maître Picot pressed my arm, and said: " Did you know that the shepherd killed his wife? "

I was dumfounded, and asked: " What? Gargan? The deaf and dumb one? "

" Yes, last winter. He was tried at Rouen. I'll tell you about it." He dragged me behind the bushes, for the dumb man could gather the words from his master's mouth as though he could hear them. He was the only man that he could understand; but in front of him he was no longer deaf, and the master, on the other hand, could guess like a sorcerer every intention of the dumb man's pantomime, every motion of his fingers, every wrinkle of his face and glance of his eyes.

Here is this simple story, a somber tragedy such as sometimes happens in the country:

Gargan was the son of a marl-digger, one of these men who go down into the marl pits in order to extract this soft, white, crumbling rock, which is then scattered over the fields. He was deaf and dumb at birth, and had been brought up to herd beasts. Then, when Picot's father took him in, he became the shepherd of the farm. He was an excellent shepherd, devoted and honest, and he knew how to heal broken members, although nobody had ever taught him anything about that. When Picot took the farm Gargan was thirty. He was tall and thin, and wore the beard of a patriarch.

At about this time a poor old woman, by the name of Martel, died, leaving a fifteen-year-old girl, who was called " Brandy " on account of her inordinate love for this drink.

Picot took in this girl and employed her to do

little things, feeding her free, in exchange for her
work. She would sleep in the carriage house, in
the stable, on the straw, or on the dungheap;
everywhere and anywhere, with any one, perhaps
with the truck driver or with the hodman. But soon
she began to be seen regularly in the company of
the deaf man. How did these two wretches unite?
How did they understand each other? Had he ever
known a woman before this one—he who had never
spoken to anybody? Was it she who first went to
his rolling hut and seduced him, an Eve of the roadside? No one knows. It is only known that one day
they began to live together as husband and wife.
Nobody was surprised. And Picot even found this
quite natural.

But the priest heard of this union without con-
secration, and grew angry. He reproached Madame
Picot, worried her conscience, threatened her with
mysterious punishments. What was to be done? It
was quite simple. They would be married in the
church and by the Mayor. Neither of them had anything: he did not own a whole pair of trousers;
she did not have a skirt that hung together. Therefore nothing could stand in the way of satisfying
religion and the law. They were united in an hour,
before Mayor and priest, and everybody thought
that everything was for the best.

But soon it became a regular game throughout
the countryside to deceive this poor Gargan. Before they had been married nobody ever thought of
going with Brandy, and now everybody wanted her,
just as a joke. It only took a glass of brandy to per-
suade the woman to deceive her husband. The affair had gained such notoriety throughout the neighborhood that gentlemen came from Goderville to

watch the game.  For a pint Brandy would give an exhibition with anybody, in a ditch, behind a wall, while at the same time one could see Gargan standing motionless a hundred feet away, knitting his stockings and followed by his bleating herd.  And people would laugh themselves sick over the matter in every café of the neighborhood; it was the great topic of conversation.  People would greet each other by crying:  " Have you treated Brandy? " Everybody knew what that meant.

The shepherd seemed to see nothing.  But one day a fellow from Sassedille, by the name of Poirot, called Gargan's wife aside and showed her a full bottle behind a mill.  She understood and laughingly came to him.  They had hardly begun their criminal business when the shepherd fell upon them as though he had dropped from the clouds.  Poirot escaped as best he could, while the dumb man, with animal-like cries, kept squeezing his wife's throat.

The people who had been working in the fields hastened to the scene.  It was too late; her tongue was black, her eyes were popping out of her head, and blood was flowing from her nose.  She was dead.

The murderer was tried at Rouen.  As he was dumb people acted as his interpreters.  The details of the affair greatly amused the audience.  But the farmer was possessed by only one idea: to have his shepherd acquitted; and he went about the matter in a cunning manner.

He first told the whole of the deaf man's history, and that of his marriage; then he came to the crime and questioned the murderer himself.  The whole audience was silent.

Picot asked slowly:  " Did you know that she

was deceiving you?" and at the same time he repeated the question with his eyes.

The other answered: "No," with his head.

"Were you sleeping in the mill when you surprised her?" And he made the gesture of a man who sees a disgusting sight.

Then the farmer imitated the motions of the Mayor who marries and the priest who unites in the name of God, and asked his servant if he had killed his wife because she was bound to him before all men and before Heaven.

The shepherd said: "Yes," with his head.

Picot said: "Now, show us how it happened."

Then the deaf man went over the whole scene. He showed how he had been sleeping in the mill, that he had awakened when he felt something moving in the straw, that he had gently looked and had seen the thing.

He was standing between two gendarmes, and suddenly he imitated the motions of the couple before him.

A loud burst of laughter filled the courtroom, then stopped short; for the shepherd, with haggard eyes, was moving his jaws and his great beard as if he were biting something, his arms stretched out, his head shoved forward, repeating the terrible action of the murderer strangling some creature.

And he was howling frightfully, so maddened by anger that he thought that he was holding her again, and the gendarmes were obliged to force him down on a bench in order to calm him.

A thrill of anguish ran through the audience. Then Maître Pîcot placed his hand on his servant's shoulder and said quietly: "This man has honor."

The shepherd was acquitted.

For my part, my dear, I was greatly moved by the last part of this adventure, which I have told you in quite vulgar terms, in order to change nothing of the farmer's story. Suddenly I heard a shot coming from the woods, and Gaspard's rumbling voice came to me like a cannon, crying: "Woodcock!"

And that is how I spend my time watching for the woodcocks, while you go to the Bois to observe the first winter gowns.

# The Abbé Marignan

BBE MARIGNAN'S martial
name suited him well. He
was a tall, thin priest, fana-
tic, excitable, yet upright. All
his beliefs were fixed, never
varying. He believed sin-
cerely that he knew his God,
penetrated His plans, desires
and intentions.

When he walked with long
strides through the road of
his little country parsonage, he would sometimes ask
himself the question: '' Why has God done this? ''
And he would dwell on this mentally, putting himself
in the place of God, and he almost invariably found
the answer. He would never have cried out in a
frenzy of pious humility: '' Thy ways, O Lord, are
past finding out.''

He said to himself: '' I am the servant of God;
it is right for me to know the reason of His deeds,
or to guess it if I do not know it.''

Everything in nature seemed to him to have been
created in accordance with an admirable and abso-

lute logic. The "whys" and "becauses" always balanced. Dawn was given to make the awakening pleasant, the days to ripen the harvest, the rains to moisten it, the evenings for preparation for slumber, and dark nights for sleep.

The four seasons corresponded perfectly with the needs of agriculture, and no suspicion had ever come to the priest of the fact that nature has no intentions; that, on the contrary, everything which exists must conform to the hard demands of epochs, climates and matter.

But he hated woman—hated her unconsciously, and despised her by instinct. He often repeated the words of Christ: " Woman, what have I to do with thee?" and he would add: " It seems as though God Himself were dissatisfied with this work of His." She was the tempter who had led the first man astray, and who since then had ever been busy with her work of damnation, the feeble creature, dangerous and forever troubling. And even more than their sinful bodies he hated their loving hearts.

He had often felt their tenderness directed toward himself, and though he knew that he was invulnerable, he grew angry at this need of love that is always in them.

According to his belief, God had created woman for the sole purpose of tempting and proving man. One must not approach her without defensive precautions and fear of possible snares. She was, indeed, just like a snare, with her lips open and her arms stretched out to man.

He had no indulgence except for nuns, whom their vows had rendered inoffensive; but he was stern with them, nevertheless, because he felt that at the bottom of their chained and humble hearts the everlasting tenderness was burning brightly—that tenderness which was shown even to him, a priest.

He felt this cursed tenderness even in their docility, in the low tones of their voices, when speaking to him, in their lowered eyes, and in their resigned tears when he reproved them roughly. And he would shake his cassock on leaving the convent doors, and walk off, lengthening his stride as though flying from danger.

He had a niece who lived with her mother in a little house near him. He was bent upon making a sister of charity of her.

She was a pretty, mocking madcap. When the abbé preached she laughed, and when he was angry with her she embraced him tightly, drawing him to her heart, while he sought unconsciously to release himself from this embrace, which nevertheless filled him with a sweet pleasure, awakening in his depths the sensation of paternity which slumbers in every man.

Often, when walking by her side, along the road, between the fields, he spoke to her of God, of his God. She never listened to him, but looked about her at the sky, the grass and flowers, and in her eyes shone the joy of life for everyone to see. At times she would jump forward to catch some flying creature, crying out as she brought it back: " Look, uncle, how pretty it is! I want to hug it! " And this desire to " hug " flies or lilac blossoms disquieted, angered, and roused the priest, who saw, even in this, the ineradicable tenderness that is always budding in women's hearts.

Then there came a day when the sexton's wife, who kept house for Abbé Marignan, told him, with caution, that his niece had a lover.

Almost suffocated by the fearful emotion this news roused in him, he stood there, his face covered with soap, for he was in the act of shaving.

When he had sufficiently recovered to think and speak, he cried: " It is not true; you lie, Mélanie! "

But the peasant woman put her hand on her heart, saying: " May our Lord judge me if I lie, Monsieur le Curé! I tell you, she goes to him every night when your sister has gone to bed. They meet by the river side; you have only to go there and see, between ten o'clock and midnight."

He ceased scraping his chin, and began to walk up and down with heavy steps, as he always did in times of deep meditation. He began shaving again and cut himself three times from his nose to his ear.

All day long he was silent, full of anger and indignation. To his priestly hatred of this invincible love was added the exasperation of her spiritual father, of her tutor and pastor deceived and played with by a child, and the selfish emotion shown by parents when their daughter announces that she has chosen a husband without them and in spite of them.

After dinner he tried to read a little, but could not, growing more and more angry. When ten o'clock struck he seized his cane, a formidable oak stick, which he was accustomed to carry in his nocturnal walks when visiting the sick. And he smiled at the enormous club which he twirled in a threatening manner in his strong, country fist. Then he raised it suddenly and, gritting his teeth, brought it down on a chair, the broken back of which fell over on the floor.

He opened the door to go out, but stopped on the sill, surprised by the splendid moonlight, of such brilliance as is seldom seen.

And, as he was gifted with an emotional nature, one such as all those poetic dreamers, the Fathers of the Church, should have, he felt suddenly distracted and moved by the grand and serene beauty of this pale night.

In his little garden, all bathed in soft light, his fruit trees in a row cast on the ground the shadow of their slim branches, scarcely clothed with verdure, while the giant honeysuckle, clinging to the wall of his house, exhaled a delicious fragrance, filling the clear, warm air with a kind of sweetened, perfumed soul.

He began to take long breaths, drinking in the air as drunkards drink wine, and he walked along slowly, delighted, marveling, almost forgetting his niece.

As soon as he was outside of the garden, he stopped to gaze upon the plain all flooded by the caressing light, bathed in the tender, languishing charm of the serene night. At each moment was heard the short, metallic note of the cricket, and distant nightingales poured out their music note by note—their light, vibrating music that sets one dreaming without thinking, made for kisses, for the seduction of moonlight.

The abbé walked on again, his heart failing, though he knew not why. He seemed weakened, suddenly exhausted; he wanted to sit down, to rest there, to think, to admire God in His works.

Down yonder, following the undulations of the little river, a great line of poplars wound in and out. A fine mist, a white haze that the moonbeams crossed, silvered, and made shining, hung about and over the mountains, enveloping all the tortuous course of the water like a kind of light and transparent cotton.

The priest stopped once again, his soul filled by a growing and irresistible tenderness.

And a doubt, a vague feeling of disquiet came over him; he was asking one of those questions that he sometimes put to himself.

"Why did God make this? Since the night is destined for sleep, unconsciousness, repose, forgetfulness of everything, why make it more charming than day, softer than dawn or evening? And why this seductive planet, more poetic than the sun, that seems destined, so discreet is it, to illuminate things too delicate and mysterious for the great light, that makes so transparent the shadows?

"Why does not the greatest of bird-singers sleep like the others? Why does it pour forth its voice in this mysterious shade?

"Why this half-veil cast over the world? Why these tremblings of the heart, this emotion of the spirit, this languishing of the body? Why this display of seductions that men do not see, since they are lying in their beds? For whom is destined this sublime spectacle, this abundance of poetry cast from heaven to earth?"

And the abbé could not understand.

But see, out there, on the edge of the meadow, under the arch of trees bathed in a shining mist, two figures are walking side by side.

The man was the taller, and held his arm about his sweetheart's neck and kissed her brow every little while. They imparted life to the placid landscape that enveloped them as a frame worthy of them. The two seemed but a single being, the being for whom was destined this calm and silent night, and they came toward the priest as a living answer, the response his Master sent to his query.

He stood still, his heart beating, all upset, and it seemed to him that he was beholding some biblical scene, like the loves of Ruth and Boaz, the accomplishment of the will of the Lord, in one of those glorious stories of which the sacred books tell. The verses of the Song of Songs began to ring in his ears, the cries of ardor, all the poetry of this poem of love.

And he said unto himself: "Perhaps God has made such nights as these to veil the ideal of the love of men."

He shrank back from this couple that still advanced with arms intertwined. Yet it was his niece. But he asked himself now if he would not be disobeying God. And does not God permit love, since He surrounds it with such visible splendor?

And he went back musing, almost ashamed, as if he had penetrated into a temple where he had no right to enter.

# On the Railway

T HE sun was about to disappear behind the great chain of mountains of which the Puy de Dôme is the giant, and the shadow of the peaks stretched into the Valley Royat.

A few persons were walking through the park around the bandstand; others were sitting in groups, notwithstanding the coolness of the evening. In one of these groups the conversation was animated, for the question was one which greatly bothered Mesdames de Sarcagnes, De Vaulacelles, and De Bridoie. Vacations were to begin in a few days, and they had to send for their sons, who were being educated by the Jesuits and the Dominicans.

Now, these ladies had no desire themselves to undertake a journey to fetch their descendants, and they knew of no one to whom they could intrust this delicate mission. It was the end of July. Paris was empty. They were searching in vain for a name which offered them sufficient guaranty.

Their embarrassment grew when they heard of a great breach of morality which had happened on a railway train a few days previously. And the ladies were positive that all the gay girls of the whole capital spent their lives on the expresses between Auvergne and the Lyons Station. According to M. de Bridoie, of the *Gil Blas,* all these women had gone to Vichy, Mont Doré, and Bourboule. In order to get there they must have gone on the railway, and they would again undoubtedly come back by the same means of transportation; they must probably be going back and forth every day. It was, therefore, a continual coming and going of naughty people on that confounded line. The ladies were most distressed that entrance to the stations should not be forbidden to suspicious women.

Now, Roger de Sarcagnes was fifteen, Gontran de Vaulacelles thirteen, and Roland de Bridoie eleven. What was to be done? They could not expose their dear children to the contact of such creatures. What might they not hear? What might they not learn if they were to spend a whole day or night in a compartment which contained one or two of these persons, with a couple of their companions?

The situation seemed to be absolutely hopeless, when Madame de Martinsec happened to pass. She stopped to greet her friends, who told her their troubles.

" Why, the matter is quite simple," she exclaimed. " I will lend you the Abbé. I can very well get along without him for forty-eight hours. Rodolphe's education will not be compromised by that. He can go for your children and bring them back again.''

Thus it was agreed upon that Abbé Lecuir, a well-educated young priest, Rodolphe de Martinsec's tutor, should go to Paris the following week in order to fetch the three boys.

The Abbé left on Friday, and on Sunday morning he was at the Lyons Station, ready to take the eight-o'clock train with his three boys. This was a new express, which had been organized for only a few days by request of all the Auvergne bathers.

He was walking along, followed by his brood, and looking for an empty compartment, or for one occupied by respectable-looking people, for his mind was haunted by all the minute warnings of Mesdames de Sarcagnes, De Vaulacelles, and De Bridoie.

Suddenly he noticed an old gentleman and a white-haired old lady, who were talking to another lady already settled in the compartment. The old gentleman was an officer of the Legion of Honor, and these people looked quite respectable. '' This is what I want,'' thought the Abbé. He told the three boys to go in, and followed them.

The old lady was saying: '' Be sure to take care, my child.''

The young one answered: '' Oh! yes, mamma, fear nothing.''

'' Call the doctor as soon as you feel sick.''

'' Yes, yes, mamma.''

'' Good-by, my child.''

'' Good-by, mamma.''

After lengthy farewells a conductor closed the doors, and the train started.

They were alone. The delighted Abbé was congratulating himself on his skill, and he began to talk to the young people who had been confided to his care. It had been decided on the day of his departure that Madame de Martinsec would allow him to give lessons to these three boys during the vacations, and he wished to test the intelligence and character of his new scholars.

The oldest one, Roger de Sarcagnes, was one of these tall schoolboys who have grown beyond their age, thin and pale, and whose pronunciation did not yet seem to be quite settled. He spoke slowly and simply.

Gontran de Vaulacelles, on the contrary, was short and stocky, and he was tricky, sly, bad, and mischievous. He was continually making fun of everybody, spoke like a grown person, and said things with double meanings, which worried his parents.

The youngest lad, Roland de Bridoie, seemed to show no special aptitude for anything. He was a harmless little creature, who would some day resemble his father.

The Abbé had informed them that they would be under his orders during these two summer months; and he had given them a little lecture on their duties toward him, the policy he should pursue, and the method he should employ with them. He was an honest-hearted and simple priest, with a mind full of systems.

His speech was interrupted by a deep sigh from his neighbor. He turned and looked at her. She was in her corner, her eyes fixed on the floor, her cheeks a little pale. The Abbé returned to his pupils.

The train was rolling along at full speed, through fields and forests, passing under and over bridges, shaking up the little company of travelers shut up in the compartments.

Gontran de Vaulacelles was now questioning Abbé Lecuir about Royat as to what amusement could be found in the country. Was there a river? How was the fishing? Should he have a horse, as he had had the year before?

The young woman suddenly uttered a sharp cry, an " Ah! " of suffering, quickly repressed.

The priest anxiously asked her: " Are you feeling ill, Madame? "

She answered: " No, no, Monsieur l'Abbé, it's nothing at all, just a slight pain. I have not been well for the last few days, and the motion of the train tires me."

Her face had indeed become quite livid. He insisted: " If I can do anything at all for you, Madame——"

" Oh! no, nothing at all, thank you, Monsieur l'Abbé."

The priest again took up his conversation with his pupils, preparing them for the instructions they were to receive under his direction.

Hours rolled by. The train stopped from time to time, and then started again. The young woman now appeared to be asleep and she was no longer moving, huddled up in her corner. Although the day was half over, she had as yet eaten nothing. The Abbé thought: " This person must be quite ill."

Only two hours remained before they were due to arrive at Clermont-Ferrand, when the woman suddenly began to moan. She had almost fallen from her seat, and, leaning against her hands, her eyes haggard, her features contorted, she kept repeating: " Oh! my God! Oh! my God! "

The Abbé rushed to her aid, exclaiming: "Madame! Madame! Madame, what is the matter?"

She stammered: "I—I—I think that—that I am going to give birth!" And she immediately began to shriek in a frightful manner. She let out a maddening cry which seemed to rasp her throat, shrill and terrible, which told of the agony of her soul and the torture of her body.

The poor priest stood bewildered before her, not knowing what to do, to say, to attempt, and he kept murmuring: "Gracious! if I only knew—gracious, if I only knew!" He had blushed to the tips of his ears, and his three pupils looked in a dazed manner at this prostrate, shrieking woman.

Suddenly she twisted, raised her arms over her head, and seemed to be shaken by a strange convulsion.

The Abbé thought that she was about to die—die beside him, deprived of aid and assistance, by his fault. Then he said in a resolute voice:

"I will help you, Madame. I do not know—but I will help you as best I can. I owe my assistance to every suffering creature."

Then he turned around to the three youngsters and cried: "You boys are to stick your heads out of the window, and if one of you turns around he shall copy a thousand lines of Virgil."

He lowered the three windows and stuck the three heads through them and pulled the shades down; then he repeated: "If you make one single motion you shall be deprived of your excursions throughout all the holidays. And do not forget that I never forgive."

Rolling up the sleeves of his cassock, he returned to the young woman.

She was still moaning, and at times shrieking.
The Abbé, with a pained expression, kept assisting
her, exhorting her and comforting her, and he continually kept one eye on the three youngsters, who
were casting quick and secret glances toward the
mysterious business which was being carried on by
their new tutor.

"Monsieur de Vaulacelles, you will copy the
verb ' to disobey ' twenty times! " he cried.

"Monsieur de Bridoie, you shall have no dessert for a month! "

Suddenly the young woman stopped her com-
plaining, and almost immediately a strange and faint
cry, like that of a cat, caused the three schoolboys
to turn around with a start, convinced that they
had heard a new-born puppy.

The Abbé was holding in his hands a tiny naked
infant. He was looking around with a bewildered
expression; he seemed pleased and sad, ready to
laugh and cry; the facial expression varied so suddenly that one might have thought him to be a
lunatic.

He announced to his pupils, as if it were a great
piece of news: "It's a boy."

Then immediately he continued: "Monsieur de
Sarcagnes, pass me the bottle of water which is in
the net. Very well. Open it. Good. Pour just a
few drops in my hand, just a few—that's enough! "

And he poured this water over the bare brow
of the little creature which he was holding in his
arms; then he said: "I baptize you in the name of
the Father and of the Son and of the Holy Ghost.
Amen."

The train was rolling into the station of Cler-
mont. Madame de Bridoie's face appeared at the

door. Then the Abbé completely lost his head and presented to her the frail human creature, murmuring: "Madame has just had a little accident during the journey."

He looked as if he had picked this child up out of the gutter. Perspiration was standing out on his brow, and his cassock was all rumpled up. He kept repeating: "They saw nothing—nothing at all—I guarantee it. All three of them were looking through the window. I guarantee it—they saw nothing at all."

And he left the compartment with four boys, instead of the three which he had been sent to fetch; while Mesdames de Bridoie, De Vaulacelles, and De Sarcagnes, livid, exchanged bewildered looks, without finding a single thing to say.

That evening the three families were dining together in order to celebrate the return of the schoolboys. The conversation lagged; fathers, mothers, and even the children themselves looked preoccupied.

Suddenly the youngest one, Roland de Bridoie, asked:

"Say, mamma, where did the Abbé find the little boy?"

The mother merely answered. "Eat your dinner, and don't trouble us with your questions."

He was silent for a short while, and then continued: "There was nobody but this lady, who had a stomach-ache. The Abbé must be a prestidigitator like Robert Houdin, who brings a bowl full of fishes from under a handkerchief."

"Keep quiet. It was God who sent it."

"But where did God put it? I didn't see anything. Did he come in through the window?"

Madame de Bridoie impatiently answered:
" Oh, be still. The stork brought him, as he does all
other children. You know it very well."

" But there wasn't any stork on the train! "

Then Gontran de Vaulacelles, who had been listening, smiled slyly and said: " Yes, there was a
stork. But Monsieur l'Abbé was the only one who
saw it."

## Madame Baptiste

HE first thing I did was to look at the clock as I entered the waiting-room of the station at Loubain, and I found that I had to wait two hours and ten minutes for the Paris express.

I had walked twenty miles and felt suddenly tired. Not seeing anything on the station walls to amuse me, I went outside and stood there racking my brains to think of something to do. The street was a kind of boulevard, planted with acacias, and on either side a row of houses of varying shape and different styles of architecture, houses such as one only sees in a small town, and ascended a slight hill, at the extreme end of which there were some trees, as though it ended in a park.

From time to time a cat crossed the street and jumped over the gutters, carefully. A cur sniffed

at every tree and hunted for scraps from the kitch-
ens, but I did not see a single human being, and I
felt listless and disheartened.   What could I do
with myself?   I was already thinking of the inevi-
table and interminable visit to the small café at the
railway station, where I should have to sit over a
glass of undrinkable beer and the illegible news-
paper, when I saw a funeral procession coming out
of a side street into the one in which I was, and the
sight of the hearse was a relief to me.   It would,
at any rate, give me something to do for ten minutes.   Suddenly, however, my curiosity was aroused.
The hearse was followed by eight gentlemen, one of
whom was weeping, while the others were chatting
together, but there was no priest, and I thought to
myself:

" This is a non-religious funeral; " and then I
reflected that a town like Loubain must contain at
least a hundred freethinkers, who would have made
a point of making a manifestation.   What could it
be, then?   The rapid pace of the procession clearly
proved that the body was to be buried without ceremony, and, consequently, without the intervention
of the Church.

My idle curiosity framed the most complicated
surmises, and as the hearse passed me, a strange
idea struck me, which was to follow it, with the
eight gentlemen.   That would take up my time for
an hour, at least, and I, accordingly, walked with
the others, with a sad look on my face, and, on seeing this, the two last turned round in surprise, and
then spoke to each other in a low voice.

No doubt, they were asking each other whether
I belonged to the town, and then they consulted the
two in front of them, who stared at me in turn.

This close scrutiny annoyed me, and to put an end to it, I went up to them, and, after bowing, I said:

" I beg your pardon, gentlemen, for interrupting your conversation, but, seeing a civil funeral, I have followed it, although I did not know the deceased gentleman whom you are accompanying."

" It was a woman," one of them said.

I was much surprised at hearing this, and asked: " But it is a civil funeral, is it not? "

The other gentleman, who evidently wished to tell me all about it, then said: " Yes and no. The clergy have refused to allow us the use of the church."

On hearing this, I uttered a prolonged " A—h! " of astonishment. I could not understand it at all, but my obliging neighbor continued:

" It is rather a long story. This young woman committed suicide, and that is the reason why she cannot be buried with any religious ceremony. The gentleman who is walking first, and who is crying, is her husband."

I replied, with some hesitation:

"You surprise and interest me very much, Monsieur. Shall I be indiscreet if I ask you to tell me the facts of the case? If I am troubling you, forget that I have said anything about the matter."

The gentleman took my arm familiarly.

" Not at all, not at all. Let us linger a little behind the others, and I will tell it you, although it is a very sad story. We have plenty of time before getting to the cemetery, the trees of which you see up yonder, for it is a stiff pull up this hill."

And he began:

" This young woman, Madame Paul Hamot, was the daughter of a wealthy merchant in the neighborhood, Monsieur Fontanelle. When she was a mere child of eleven, she had a terrible adventure; a footman attacked her and she nearly died. A terrible criminal case was the result, and the man was sentenced to penal servitude for life.

" The little girl grew up, stigmatized by disgrace, isolated, without any companions, and grown-up people would scarcely kiss her, for they thought that they would soil their lips if they touched her forehead, and she became a sort of monster, a phenomenon to all the town. People said to each other in a whisper: ' You know, little Fontanelle,' and everybody turned away in the streets when she passed. Her parents could not even get a nurse to take her out for a walk, as the other servants held aloof from her, as if contact with her would poison everybody who came near her.

" It was pitiable to see the poor child go and play every afternoon. She remained quite by herself, standing by her maid, and looking at the other children amusing themselves. Sometimes, yielding to an irresistible desire to mix with the other children, she advanced timidly, with nervous gestures, and mingled with a group, with furtive steps, as if conscious of her own disgrace. And, immediately, the mothers, aunts, and nurses would come running from every seat, and take the children intrusted to their care by the hand and drag them brutally away.

" Little Fontanelle remained isolated, wretched, without understanding what it meant, and then she began to cry, nearly heartbroken with grief, and then she used to run and hide her head in her nurse's lap, sobbing.

" As she grew up, it was worse still. They kept the girls from her, as if she were stricken with the plague. Remember that she had nothing to learn, nothing; that she no longer had the right to the symbolical wreath of orange-flowers; that almost before she could read she had penetrated that redoubtable mystery which mothers scarcely allow their daughters to guess at, trembling as they enlighten them on the night of their marriage.

" When she went through the streets, always accompanied by her governess, as if her parents feared some fresh, terrible adventure, with her eyes cast down under the load of that mysterious disgrace which she felt was always weighing upon her, the other girls, who were not nearly so innocent as people thought, whispered and giggled as they looked at her knowingly, and immediately turned their heads absently, if she happened to look at them. People scarcely greeted her; only a few men bowed to her, and the mothers pretended not to see her, while some young blackguards called her Madame Baptiste, after the name of the footman who had attacked her.

" Nobody knew the secret torture of her mind, for she hardly ever spoke, and never laughed, and her parents themselves appeared uncomfortable in her presence, as if they bore her a constant grudge for some irreparable fault.

" An honest man would not willingly give his hand to a liberated convict, would he, even if that convict were his own son? And Monsieur and Madame Fontanelle looked on their daughter as they would have done on a son who had just been released from the hulks. She was pretty and pale, tall, slender, distinguished-looking, and she would have pleased me very much, Monsieur, but for that unfortunate affair.

" Well, when a new sub-prefect was appointed
here, eighteen months ago, he brought his private
secretary with him. He was a queer sort of fellow,
who had lived in the Latin Quarter, it appears. He
saw Mademoiselle Fontanelle, and fell in love with
her, and when told of what had occurred, he merely
said: ' Bah! That is just a guarantee for the future, and I would rather it should have happened
before I married her than afterward. I shall live
tranquilly with that woman.'

" He paid his addresses to her, asked for her
hand, and married her, and then, not being deficient
in assurance, he paid wedding-calls, as if nothing
had happened. Some people returned them, others
did not; but, at last, the affair began to be forgotten,
and she took her proper place in society.

" She adored her husband as if he had been a
god; for, you must remember, he had restored her
to honor and to social life, had braved public opinion, faced insults, and, in a word, performed such a
courageous act as few men would undertake, and
she felt the most exalted and tender love for him.

" When she became *enceinte,* and it was known,
the most particular people and the greatest sticklers
opened their doors to her, as if she had been definitely purified by maternity.

" It is strange, but so it is, and thus everything
was going on as well as possible until the other day,
which was the feast of the patron saint of our town.
The Prefect, surrounded by his staff and the au-
thorities, presided at the musical competition, and
when he had finished his speech the distribution of
medals began, which Paul Hamot, his private secretary, handed to those who were entitled to them.

" As you know, there are always jealousies and

rivalries, which make people forget all propriety. All the ladies of the town were there on the platform, and, in his turn, the bandmaster from the village of Mourmillon came up. This band was only to receive a second-class medal, for one cannot give first-class medals to everybody, can one? But when the private secretary handed him his badge, the man threw it in his face and exclaimed:

" ' You may keep your medal for Baptiste. You owe him a first-class one, also, just as you do me.'

" There were a number of people there who began to laugh. The common herd are neither charitable nor refined, and every eye was turned toward that poor lady. Have you ever seen a woman going mad, Monsieur? Well, we were present at the sight! She got up, and fell back on her chair three times in succession, as if she wished to make her escape, but saw that she could not make her way through the crowd, and then another voice in the crowd exclaimed:

" ' Oh! Oh! Madame Baptiste! '

" And a great uproar, partly of laughter and partly of indignation, arose. The word was repeated over and over again; people stood on tiptoe to see the unhappy woman's face; husbands lifted their wives up in their arms, so that they might see her, and people asked:

" ' Which is she? The one in blue? '

" The boys crowed like cocks, and laughter was heard all over the place.

" She did not move now on her state chair, but sat just as if she had been put there for the crowd to look at. She could not move, nor conceal herself, nor hide her face. Her eyelids blinked quickly, as if a vivid light were shining on them, and she breathed heavily like a horse that is going up a steep hill, so that it almost broke one's heart to see her. Meanwhile, however, Monsieur Hamot had seized the ruffian by the throat, and they were rolling on the ground together, amid a scene of confusion, and the ceremony was interrupted.

" An hour later, as the Hamots were returning home, the young woman, who had not uttered a word since the insult, but who was trembling as if all her nerves had been set in motion by springs, suddenly sprang over the parapet of the bridge, and threw herself into the river, before her husband could prevent her. The water is very deep under the arches, and it was two hours before her body was recovered. Of course, she was dead."

The narrator stopped, and then added:

" It was, perhaps, the best thing she could do under the circumstances. There are some things which cannot be wiped out, and now you understand why the clergy refused to have her taken into church. Ah! If it had been a religious funeral the whole town would have been present, but you can understand that her suicide added to the other affair and made families abstain from attending her funeral; and then, it is not an easy matter here to attend a funeral which is performed without religious rites."

We passed through the cemetery gates and I waited, much moved by what I had heard, until the coffin had been lowered into the grave, before I went up to the poor fellow who was sobbing violently, to press his hand warmly. He looked at me in surprise through his tears, and then said:

" Thank you, Monsieur." And I was not sorry that I had followed the funeral.

# A Warning Note

HAVE received the following letter. Thinking that it may be profitable to many readers, I lost no time in communicating to them its contents:

" PARIS, November 15th, 1886.

" MONSIEUR: You often, either in the form of short stories or chronicles, deal with subjects relating to what I may describe as ' current morals.' I am going to submit to you some reflections which ought, it seems to me, to furnish you with the materials for one of your tales.

" I am not married; I am a bachelor, and, as it seems to me, a rather simple man. But I fancy that many men, the greater number of men, are simple in the way that I am. Acting always, or nearly always, in good faith myself, I am unable to understand the inherent astuteness of my neighbors, and I look straight before me as I proceed, without being sufficiently on my guard against hidden motives, secret actions.

" We are nearly all accustomed as a rule to take

things as they appear, and to take people at their
own valuation; and very few possess that percep-
tion which enables certain men to divine the real
and hidden nature of others.  From this peculiar
and conventional attitude in regard to life we have
come to this, that we pass like moles through the
midst of events, and that we never believe in what
really is, but in what appears to be, that as soon as
we are shown the fact behind the veil we declare
that it is not true to life, and that everything which
displeases our idealistic morality is classed by us as
an exception, without taking into account that these
exceptions all brought together constitute nearly
the sum total of cases.  Another result of this is
that credulous good people like me are deceived by
everybody, and especially by women, who have a
talent in this direction.

  " I have started far afield in order to come to
the particular fact which interests me.  I have a
sweetheart, a married woman.  Like many others, I
imagined, of course, that I had chanced on an exception, on an unhappy little woman who was deceiving her husband for the first time.  I had paid
attentions to her, or, rather, I had looked on myself
as having paid attention to her for a long time, as
having overcome her scruples by dint of kindness
and love, and as having triumphed by the sheer
force of perseverance.  In fact, I had made use of a
thousand precautions, a thousand devices, and a
thousand subtle dallyings in order to succeed in getting the better of her.

  " Now, here is what happened last week:  Her
husband being absent for some days, she suggested
that we should both dine together, and that I should
wait on myself so as to avoid the presence of a man-

servant. She had a fixed idea which had haunted
her for the last four or five months: She wanted to
become intoxicated, without being afraid of conse-
quences, without having to go back home, or to
speak to her chambermaid and to walk before witnesses. She had often taken a little too much without going farther, and she had enjoyed it. So she
promised herself that she would become intoxicated
for once, only once, but thoroughly so. She pretended at her own house that she was going to spend
twenty-four hours with some friends near Paris,
and she reached my abode just about dinner-hour.

" A woman naturally ought not to get drunk on
anything but champagne frappé. She drank a large
glass of it fasting, and before the oysters were
served she was talking incoherently.

" We had a cold dinner spread on a table behind me. All I had to do was to reach out my arm
and take the dishes or plates, and I did the honors
indifferently well as I listened to her chattering.

" She kept taking swallows, haunted by her fixed
idea. She began by making me the recipient of
meaningless and interminable confidences about her
sensations as a young girl. She went on and on,
her eyes wandering and sparkling, her tongue
loosed, as her frivolous ideas poured forth just
as tape is rolled off a ticker.

" From time to time she asked me:

" ' Am I tipsy? '

" ' No, not yet.'

" And she went on drinking.

" She was so before long, not so as to lose her
senses, but tipsy enough to tell the truth, as it
seemed to me.

" Her confidences as to her emotions while a

young girl were succeeded by more intimate confidences as to her relations with her husband. She
made them without restraint till I was embarrassed,
saying continually: ' I can tell everything to you.
To whom could I tell everything if it were not to
you? ' So I was made acquainted with all the habits,
all the defects, all the fads and the most secret in-
clinations of her husband.

" And by way of claiming my approval she
asked: ' Isn't he a duffer? Do you think he can
get ahead of me, eh? And the first time I saw you,
I said to myself, ' Let me see! I like him, and I'll
take him for my lover. It was then you began paying me attention.'

" I must have presented an odd appearance, for
she burst out laughing, exclaiming: ' Oh, you big
simpleton, you did go about it cautiously; but when
men pay us attention, you old stupid, it is because
we permit it. A man must be a fool not to understand, by a mere glance at us, that we mean " Yes."
Ah! I believe I waited for you, booby! Oh! yes,
flowers, verses, compliments, more verses, and nothing else! I was very near letting you go, my fine
fellow, you were so long in making up your mind.
And only to think that half the men in the world
are like you, while the other half, ha! ha! ha!'

" This laugh of hers sent a cold shiver down my
back. I stammered: ' The other half—what about
the other half? '

" She still went on drinking, her eyes sparkling
from the wine, her mind impelled by the imperious
necessity to tell the truth which sometimes takes
possession of drunkards.

" She replied: ' Ah! the other half makes quick
work of it—too quick; but, all the same, they are

right. There are days when we don't agree; but
there are days, too, when all goes right, in spite of
everything. . . . My dear, if you only knew how
funny it is—the way the two kinds of men act! You
see, the timid ones, such as you, you never could
imagine what sort the others are and what they do,
immediately, as soon as they find themselves alone
with us. They are regular dare-devils! They get
many a slap in the face from us, no doubt of that,
but what does that matter? They know we're the
sort that kiss and don't tell! They know us well,
they do!'

" I stared at her with the eyes of an inquisitor,
and with a mad desire to make her speak, to learn
everything from her. How often had I put this
question to myself: ' How do the other men be-
have toward the women who belong to us?' I was
fully conscious of the fact that, from the way I saw
two men talking to the same woman publicly in a
drawing-room, these two men, if they found themselves, one after the other, all alone with her, would
conduct themselves quite differently, although they
were both equally well acquainted with her. We
can guess at the first glance of the eye that certain
beings, naturally endowed with the power of seduction, or, perhaps, more lively, more daring than
we are, attain after an hour's chat with a woman
who pleases them a degree of intimacy that we
would not hope for in a year. Well, these men, these
seducers, these bold adventurers, when the occasion
presents itself to them, take liberties which we timid
ones would consider odious outrages, but which
women, perhaps, look on merely as pardonable ef-
frontery, as indecent homage to their irresistible
grace.

" So I asked her: ' There are some men, are there not, who are very improper? '

" She threw herself back in her chair in order to laugh more at her ease, but with a nervous, unhealthy laugh, one of those laughs which ends in an attack of nerves; then, a little more calmly, she replied: ' Ha! ha! my dear,·improper? That is to say, that they dare everything at once, all, you understand, and many other things, too.'

" I felt disgusted as if she had just revealed to me a monstrous thing.

" ' And you permit this, you women? '

" ' No, we don't permit it; we slap them in the face, but, for all that, they amuse us! And then with them one is always afraid, one is never easy. You must keep watching them the whole time; it is like fighting a duel. You have to keep staring into their eyes to see what they are thinking of or where they are putting their hands. They are blackguards, if you like, but they love us better than you do.'

" A singular and unexpected sensation stole over me. Although a bachelor and determined to remain a bachelor, I suddenly felt in my breast the spirit of a husband in the face of this impudent confidence. I felt myself the friend, the ally, the brother of all these confiding men who are, if not robbed, at least defrauded by all these pirates.

" It is this strange emotion, Monsieur, that I am obeying at this moment, in writing to you, and in begging of you to address a warning note to the great army of easy-going husbands.

" However, I had still some lingering doubts. This woman was drunk and must be lying.

" I went on to inquire: ' How is it that you

never relate these adventures to any one, you women?'

" She gazed at me with profound pity, and with such an air of sincerity that for the moment I thought she had been sobered by astonishment.

" We—— My dear fellow, you are very foolish. Why do we never talk to you about these things? Ha! ha! ha! Does your valet tell you about his tips, his odd sous? Well, these are our little tips. The husband ought not to complain when we don't go any farther. But how stupid you are! . . . And then what harm does it do as long as we don't yield?'

" I again asked her, with much embarrassment:
" ' So then you have often been kissed by men?'

" She answered, with an air of sovereign contempt for the man who could have any doubt on the subject:

" ' Why, every woman has been often embraced. . . . Try it on with any of them, no matter whom, in order to see for yourself, you great goose! Look here! embrace Madame de X! She is quite young and very virtuous. Embrace some one, my friend—embrace and touch; you will see, ha! ha! ha!'

*　*　*　*　*　*　*

" All of a sudden she flung her glass straight at the chandelier. The champagne fell down in a shower, extinguishing three wax-candles, stained the hangings, and deluged the table, while the broken glass was scattered about the dining-room. Then she made an effort to seize the bottle to do the same with it, but I prevented her. After that, she began to scream in a shrill voice—the nervous attack had come on, as I had foreseen. . . .

" Some days later I had almost forgotten this avowal of a tipsy woman when I chanced to find myself at an evening party with this Madame de X—— whom my sweetheart had advised me to embrace. As I lived in the same neighborhood as she did, I offered to drive her to her door, for she was alone this evening. She accepted my offer.

" As soon as we were in the carriage, I said to myself: ' Come! I must try it on! ' But I had not the courage. I did not know how to make a start, how to begin the attack.

" Then, suddenly, the desperate courage of cowards came to my aid. I said to her: ' How pretty you looked this evening! '

" She replied with a laugh: ' So, then, this evening was an exception, as this is the first time you noticed it.'

" I did not know what rejoinder to make. Certainly my gallantry was not making progress. After a little reflection, however, I managed to say:

" ' No, but I never dared to tell you.'

" She was astonished.

" ' Why? '

" ' Because it is—it is a little difficult.'

" ' Difficult to tell a woman that she's pretty? Why, where did you come from? You should always tell us so, even when you only half think it, because it always gives us pleasure to hear  . . .'

" I felt myself suddenly stirred by a whimsical audacity, and, catching her round the waist, I sought to kiss her.

" However, I must have been very awkward while trying not to be too rough, for she kept turning her head aside so as to avoid contact with my face, saying:

" ' Oh, no—this is rather too much—too much . . . You are too hasty! Take care of my hair. You cannot kiss a woman who has her hair dressed like mine! . . .'

" I resumed my former position in the carriage, disconcerted, unnerved by this repulse. But the carriage drew up before her gate; and as she stepped out of it, she held out her hand to me, saying in her most gracious tones:

" ' Thanks, dear Monsieur, for having seen me home . . . and don't forget my advice! '

" I saw her three days later. She had forgotten everything.

" And I, Monsieur, I am incessantly thinking of the other sort of men—the sort of men to whom a lady's coiffure is no obstacle, and who know how to take advantage of every opportunity."

# Joseph

HE little Baroness Andrée de la Fraisières and little Comtesse Noémi de Gardens were both of them drunk, quite drunk. They had dined together in the large room facing the sea. The soft breeze of a summer evening blew in at the open window, soft and fresh at the same time, a breeze that smelt of the sea. The two young women, extended in their lounging chairs, sipped their Chartreuse from time to time, as they smoked cigarettes. They were talking most confidentially, telling each other details which nothing but this charming intoxication could have permitted their pretty lips to utter. Their husbands had returned to Paris that afternoon, and had left them alone on that deserted little sea beach, which they had selected so as to avoid those gallant marauders that are constantly met with in fashionable watering places. As they were absent five days in the week, they objected to country excursions, luncheons on the grass, swimming lessons and those sudden familiarities which spring up in the idle life of watering places. Dieppe, Etretat, Trouville seemed to them places to be avoided, and they had rented a house which had been built and abandoned by an eccentric individual in the valley of Roqueville, near Fécamp, and there they buried their wives for the whole summer.

The ladies were frankly drunk. Not knowing how to amuse themselves, the little Baroness had suggested a good dinner and champagne. To begin with, they had found great amusement in cooking this dinner themselves, and then they had eaten it merrily, and had drunk freely, in order to allay the thirst which the heat of the fire had excited. Now they were chatting and talking nonsense, while gently moistening their throats with Chartreuse. In fact, they did not in the least know any longer what they were saying.

The Countess, with her feet in the air on the back of a chair, was further gone than her friend.

" To complete an evening like this," she said, " we ought to have a lover apiece. If I had foreseen this some time ago, I would have sent for a couple from Paris, and I would have let you have one. . . ." " I can always find one," the other replied; " I could have one this very evening, if I wished." " What nonsense! At Roqueville, my dear? It would have to be some peasant, then." " No, not altogether." " Well, tell me all about it." " What do you want me to tell you? " " About your lover? " " My dear, I do not want to live without being loved, for I should fancy I was dead

if I were not loved." "So should I." "Is not
that so?" "Yes. Men cannot understand it!
And especially our husbands!" "No, not in the
least. How can you expect it to be different? The
love which we want is made up of being spoiled,
of gallantries and of pretty words and actions.
That is the nourishment of our hearts; it is indispensable to our life, indispensable, indispensable."

"Indispensable."

"I must feel that somebody is thinking of me,
always, everywhere. When I go to sleep and when
I wake up, I must know that somebody loves me
somewhere, that I am being dreamed of, longed for.
Without that, I should be wretched, wretched! Oh!
yes, unhappy enough to do nothing but cry." "I
am just the same."

"You must remember that anything else is impossible. When a husband has been nice for six
months, or a year, or two years, he necessarily becomes a brute, yes, a regular brute. . . . He does
not put himself out for anything, but shows himself
just as he is, and makes a scene on the slightest
provocation, or without any provocation whatever.
One cannot love a man with whom one lives constantly." "That is quite true." "Isn't it? . . .
What was I saying? I cannot the least remember?" "You were saying that all husbands are
brutes!" "Yes, brutes . . . all of them."
"That is quite true." "And then?" "What do
you mean?" "What was I saying just then?"
"I don't know because you did not say it!" "But
I had something to tell you." "Oh! yes, that is
true; well? . . ." "Oh! I have got it. . . ."
"Well, I am listening." "I was telling you that
I can find lovers everywhere." "How do you man-

age it? " " Like this. Now follow me carefully.
When I get to some fresh place I take notes and
make my choice." " You make your choice? "
" Yes, of course I do. First of all I take notes. I
ask questions. Above all, a man must be discreet,
rich, and generous; is not that so? " " It is quite
true! " " And then he must please me, as a man."
" Of course." " Then I bait the hook for him."
" You bait the hook? " " Yes, just as one does to
catch fish. Have you never fished with a hook and
line? " " No, never." " That is a mistake; it is
very amusing, and besides that, it is instructive.
Well, then, I bait the hook. . . ." " How do you
do it? " " How stupid you are! Does not one catch
the man one wants to catch, without their having
any choice? And they really think that they choose
. . . the fools . . . but it is we who choose
. . . always. . . . Just think, when one is not
ugly nor stupid, as is the case with us, all men
aspire to us, all . . . without exception. We look
them over from morning till night, and when we
have selected one, we fish for him. . . ." " But
that does not tell me how you do it? " " How I
do it? . . . Why, I do nothing; I allow myself
to be looked at, that is all." " You allow yourself
to be looked at? . . ." " Why, yes; that is quite
enough. When one has allowed one's self to be
looked at several times following, a man immediately thinks you the most lovely, most seductive of
women, and then he begins to make love to you.
I give him to understand that he is not so bad-looking, without saying anything to him, of course, and
he falls in love, like a log. I have him fast, and
it lasts a longer or a shorter time, according to his
qualities."

" And do you catch all whom you please, like
that? " " Nearly all." " Oh! So there are some
who resist? " " Sometimes." " Why? " " Oh!
Why? A man is a Joseph for three reasons. Because he is in love with another woman, because
he is excessively timid, or because he is . . . how
shall I say it? . . . incapable of carrying out the
conquest of a woman to the end. . . ." " Oh!
my dear! . . . Do you really believe? . . ."
" I am sure of it . . . there are many of this
latter class, many, many . . . many more than
people think. Oh! they look just like everybody
else . . . they strut like peacocks. . . . No,
when I said peacocks . . . I made a mistake, for
they could not display themselves." " Oh! my dear.
. . ." " As to the timid, they are sometimes un-
speakably stupid. They are the sort of men who
ought not to undress themselves, even when they
are going to bed alone, when there is a looking-glass
in their room. With them, one must be energetic,
make use of looks, and squeeze their hands, and
even that is useless sometimes. They never know
how or where to begin. When one faints in their
presence . . . as a last resource . . . they try
to bring you round . . . and if you do not re-
cover your senses immediately . . . they go and
get assistance.

" Those whom I prefer myself are other wom-
en's lovers. I carry them by assault . . . at
. . . at . . . at the point of the bayonet, my
dear! " " That is all very well, but when there
are no men, as here, for instance? " " I find
them." " You find them? But where? " " Everywhere. But that reminds me of my story.

" Now, listen. Just two years ago, my husband

made me pass the summer on his estate at Bou-
grolles. There was nothing there . . . you know
what I mean, nothing, nothing, nothing whatever!
In the neighboring country houses there were a few
disgusting boors, who cared for nothing but shooting, and who lived in country houses which had not
even a bathroom, men who perspire, go to bed covered with perspiration, and whom it would be impossible to improve, because their principles of life
are dirty.  Now just guess what I did!"  "I cannot possibly."  "Ha! ha! ha!  I had just been
reading a number of George Sand's novels which
exalt the man of the people, novels in which the
workingmen are sublime and all the men of the
world are criminals.  In addition to this, I had seen
*Ruy Blas* the winter before, and it had impressed
me very much.  Well, one of our farmers had a son,
a good-looking young fellow of two and twenty who
had studied for a priest, but had left the seminary
in disgust.  Well, I took him as footman!"  "Oh!
. . . And then? . . . What afterward?"

"Then . . . then, my dear, I treated him very
haughtily, and showed him a good deal of my person.  I did not lure this rustic on, I simply inflamed
him! . . ."  "Oh! Andrée!"  "Yes, and I enjoyed the fun very much.  People say that servants
count for nothing!  Well, he did not count for much.
I used to ring to give him his orders every morning while my maid was dressing me, and every
evening as well, while she was undressing me.

"My dear, he caught fire like a thatched roof.
Then, at meals, I used continually to talk about
cleanliness, about taking care of one's person, about
baths and shower baths, until at the end of a fort-
night he bathed in the river morning and night, and

used to perfume himself enough to poison the whole château. I was even obliged to forbid him to use perfumes, telling him, with furious looks, that men ought never to use anything but eau de Cologne."

" Oh! Andrée! "

" Then, I took it into my head to get together a library suitable to the country. I sent for a few hundred moral novels, which I lent to all our peasants and all my servants. A few books . . . a few . . . poetical books . . . such as excite the mind of . . . schoolboys and schoolgirls . . . had found their way into my collection . . . and I gave them to my footman. That taught him life . . . a funny sort of life." " Oh! Andrée! "

" Then I grew familiar with him, and used to say thou to him. I had given him the name of Joseph. And, my dear, he was in a state . . . in a terrible state. . . . He got as thin as . . . as a barn-door cock . . . and rolled his eyes like an idiot. I was extremely amused; it was one of the most delightful summers I ever spent. . . ." " And then? . . ." " Then? . . . Oh! yes. . . . Well, one day when my husband was away from home, I told him to order the basket phaeton and to drive me into the woods. It was warm, very warm. . . . There! " " Oh, Andrée, do tell me all about it. . . . It is so amusing. . . ." " Here, have a glass of Chartreuse, otherwise I shall empty the decanter myself. Well, I felt ill, on the road." " How? " " You are very stupid. I told him that I was not feeling well, and that he must lay me on the grass, and when I was lying there I told him I was choking, and that he must unlace me. And then, when I was unlaced, I

fainted." "Did you go right off?" "Oh! dear
no, not the least." "Well?"

"Well, I was obliged to remain unconscious for
nearly an hour, as he could find no means of bringing me round. But I was very patient, and did
not open my eyes."

"Oh! Andrée! . . . And what did you say
to him?" "I? Nothing at all! How was I to
know anything, as I was unconscious? I thanked
him, and told him to help me into the carriage, and
he drove me back to the château; but he nearly upset us in turning into the gate!" "Oh! Andrée!
And is that all? . . ." "That is all. . . ."
"You did not faint more than that once?" "Only
once, of course! I did not want to take such a fellow for my lover." "Did you keep him long after
that?" "Yes, of course. I have him still. Why
should I have sent him away? I had nothing to
complain of." "Oh! Andrée! And is he in love
with you still?" "Of course he is." "Where
is he?"

The little Baroness put out her hand to the wall
and touched the electric bell, and the door opened
almost immediately, and a tall footman came in who
diffused a scent of eau de Cologne all round him.
"Joseph," she said to him, "I am afraid I am
going to faint; send my lady's maid to me."

The man stood motionless, like a soldier before
his officer, and fixed an ardent look on his mistress,
who continued: "Go quickly, you great idiot, we
are not in the wood to-day, and Rosalie will attend to me better than you would." He turned on
his heels and went, and the little Baroness asked
nervously: "But what shall you say to your
maid?" "I shall tell her what we have been doing!

No, I shall merely get her to unlace me; it will relieve my chest, for I can scarcely breathe. I am drunk . . . my dear . . . so drunk that I should fall if I were to get up from my chair."

# The Peddler

OW many fleeting associations, trifling things, chance meetings, humble dramas we have witnessed or guessed at, while our mind is still ignorant and unformed, are, as it were, guiding threads which lead it gradually to a knowledge of sad realities.

As I saunter along idly in my customary walks my mind, abstracted in endless, aimless reverie, constantly recurs to little, long-past incidents, amusing or the reverse, which rise up before me like birds in the brush.

This summer, as I was wandering along a road in Savoy overlooking the right bank of the Lake of Bourget, and as my glance lingered on that mass of water, mirror-like and of a unique shade of pale blue, as it gleamed in the rays of the setting sun, I felt my heart stirred by that emotion which I have felt since childhood for lakes, rivers, the sea.

On the other bank of the immense watery sur-

face rose the high mountain range, its base extend-
ing in one direction toward the Rhône, and in the
other toward the Bourget, beyond the line of vision,
its crest dentated like a cock's comb as far as the
last summit of the Dent du Chat. On either side
of the road grapevines, festooned from tree to
tree, smothered with their leaves the slender
branches round which they twined, and extended
across the landscape in green, yellow, and red gar-
lands, dotted with clusters of black grapes.

The road was deserted, white, and dusty. Suddenly a man emerged from the grove of large trees
that incloses the village of Saint-Innocent, and,
bending under a load, he came toward me, leaning
on a cane.

As he approached I recognized in him one of
those peddlers, or wandering merchants, who sell
small articles for a trifling amount, and there came
to my mind a reminiscence of days long past, a mere
nothing, simply an adventure that happened to me
between Argenteuil and Paris when I was twenty-
five.

All my happiness at that time consisted in boat-
ing. I had taken a room at a cheap eating house in
Argenteuil, and every evening I took the parlia-
mentary train, that long, slow train that deposits
at every station a crowd of men carrying packages;
they are heavy and corpulent, as they take no exercise, and their trousers are baggy from continually
sitting at an office desk. This train, in which I
seemed to get a whiff of the office and of official
documents, deposited me at Argenteuil. My boat
was waiting for me, ready to skim over the water,
and I rowed along rapidly, dining either at Chatou,
at Epinay, or at Saint-Ouen. When I got back I

put away my boat and started on foot for Paris with the moon shining down on me.

Well, one night on the white road I perceived in front of me a man walking. Oh! I was constantly meeting those night travelers of the Parisian suburbs so much dreaded by belated citizens. This man went on slowly before me with a heavy load on his shoulders.

I came right up to him at a rapid pace, my steps resounding on the road. He stopped and turned round; then, to avoid me, he crossed to the opposite side of the road.

As I rapidly passed him, he called out to me:

"Hullo! good evening, Monsieur."

I responded:

"Good evening, mate."

He went on:

"Are you going far?"

"I am going to Paris."

"You won't be long getting there; you're going at a good pace. As for me, I have too big a load on my shoulders to walk so quickly."

I slackened my pace. Why had this man spoken to me? What was he carrying in this big pack? Vague suspicions of crime sprang up in my mind and made me curious. The columns of the newspapers every morning contain so many accounts of crimes committed in this place, the peninsula of Gennevilliers, that some of them must be true. Such things are not invented merely to amuse readers— all this catalogue of arrests and varied misdeeds with which the reports of the law courts are filled.

However, this man's voice seemed rather timid than bold, and up to the present his manner had been more cautious than aggressive.

In my turn I began to question him:

" And you, are you going far? "

" Not farther than Asnières."

" Is Asnières your place of abode? "

" Yes, Monsieur, I am a peddler by occupation, and I live at Asnières."

He had left the sidewalk where pedestrians walk beneath the shade of the trees in the daytime and walked in the middle of the road. I did the same. We glanced suspiciously at each other, holding our sticks in our hands. When I was quite close to him I felt perfectly reassured; he apparently shared this feeling, for he asked:

" Would you mind going a little more slowly? "

" Why should I go slowly? "

" Because I don't care for this road by night. I have goods on my back, and two are always better than one. When two men are together people seldom attack them."

I felt that he was right, and that he was afraid. So I yielded to his wishes, and we walked along, side by side, this stranger and I, at one o'clock in the morning, along the road leading from Argenteuil to Asnières.

" Why are you going home so late if it is so dangerous? " I asked my companion.

He told me his history. He had not intended to return home this evening, as he had taken with him that very morning a stock of goods to last him three or four days. But he had been so fortunate in disposing of them that he found it necessary to return home at once in order to deliver next day a number of things which had been bought on credit.

He explained to me with genuine satisfaction that he was doing very well, having a talent for talking, and that while displaying some trifles while chatting he was able to dispose of many other things that were heavy to carry.

He added:

" I have a shop at Asnières. My wife keeps it."

" Ah! So you're married? "

" Yes, Monsieur, for the last fifteen months. I have a very nice wife. She'll be surprised when she sees me coming home to-night."

He then gave me an account of his marriage. He had been attentive to this girl for two years, but she had taken time to make up her mind.

She had since her childhood kept a little shop at the corner of a street, where she sold all sorts of things—ribbons, flowers in summer, and principally pretty little shoe-buckles, and many other trifles, of which, owing to the kindness of a manufacturer, she made a specialty. She was well known in Asnières as " La Bluette." This name was given to her because she often dressed in blue. And she made money, as she was very clever in everything she did. He did not think she was very well at the present moment, and believed she was *enceinte,* but he was not quite sure. Their business was prospering, and he traveled about exhibiting samples to all the small dealers in the adjoining districts. He had become a sort of traveling commission agent for some of the manufacturers, working at the same time for them and for himself.

" And you—in what business are you engaged? " he said.

I answered hesitatingly. I explained that I had a sailing-boat and two yawls in Argenteuil, that I came for a row every evening, and that, as I was fond of exercise, I sometimes walked back to Paris, where I had a profession, which I led him to infer was a lucrative one.

He remarked:

" Faith, if I had money, as you have, I wouldn't amuse myself by trudging along the roads like this at night. It isn't safe along here."

He gave me a sidelong glance, and I asked myself whether he might not, after all, be a cunning rascal, who.did not want to run any fruitless risk.

Then I felt reassured as he murmured:

" A little less quickly, if you please. This pack of mine is heavy."

The sight of a group of houses showed that we had reached Asnières.

" I am almost at home," he said. " We don't sleep in the shop; it is watched at night by a dog, but a dog who is worth four men. And then it costs too much to live in the center of the town. But listen to me, Monsieur! You have rendered me a great service, for I don't feel my mind at ease when I'm traveling with my pack along the roads. So now you must come in with me and drink a glass of mulled wine with my wife if she hasn't gone to bed, for she is a sound sleeper and doesn't like to be waked up. Besides, I'm not a bit afraid without my pack, and so I'll see you to the gates of the city with a cudgel in my hand."

I declined the invitation; he insisted on my coming in; I still held back; he pressed me with so much earnestness and evident sincerity and regret at my refusal, for he expressed himself well, asking me if I would not take a drink with him because of his occupation, that I at last yielded, and followed him along a lonely road to one of those large dilapidated houses that one sees on the outskirts of suburbs.

Arrived at the door, I hesitated. This great plaster barrack looked like a thieves' resort, like a den of highway robbers. But he made me take the lead as he pushed open a door. He guided me with his hands on my shoulders, through profound darkness, toward a stairway where I had to feel my way with my hands and feet, with a well-grounded apprehension of tumbling into some gaping cellar.

When I had reached the first landing he said to me: "Go on up! It's on the sixth story."

I searched my pockets, and, finding there a box of candle matches, I lighted the way up the ascent. He followed me, puffing beneath his pack, as he repeated:

"It's high up! It's high up!"

When we were at the top of the house he drew forth a key attached to the inside of his coat by a string, and, unlocking the door, he made me enter.

It was a little whitewashed room, with a table in the center, six chairs, and a kitchen-cupboard close to the wall.

"I am going to wake up my wife," he said; "then I am going down to the cellar to fetch some wine; it doesn't keep up here."

He went over to one of the two doors which opened out of this apartment, and called:

"Bluette! Bluette!" Bluette did not reply. He called out in a louder tone: "Bluette! Bluette!"

Then, knocking at the partition with his fist, he growled: "Will you wake up, in God's name?"

He waited, put his ear to the keyhole, and muttered, in a calmer tone: "Pooh! if she is asleep, she must be allowed to sleep! I'll go and get the wine: wait a couple of minutes for me."

He disappeared. I sat down and made the best
of it.

What had I come to this place for? All of a sudden I gave a start, for I heard people talking in low
tones, and moving about quietly, almost noiselessly,
in the room where the wife slept.

The devil! I must have fallen into a trap! How
was it she did not wake, this Bluette, at all the noise
her husband made? Perhaps it was only a signal
to say to his accomplices: "There's a mouse in
the trap. I'll watch the door; you attend to the
rest." I could hear them more distinctly; they
were turning the key in the lock. My heart beat
rapidly. I retreated to the other end of the room,
saying to myself: "Well, I must defend myself!"
and, seizing a chair by the back, I prepared for an
energetic struggle.

The door opened slightly, and a hand appeared
holding it ajar; then a head, the head of a man
wearing a hard felt hat, was pushed through the
half-open door, and I saw two eyes looking at me.
Then, so quickly that I had not time to think of de-
fending myself, the individual, the supposed criminal, a big young fellow, with bare feet and his
clothes just thrown on him, without a tie, his shoes
in his hand, a handsome fellow, truly, almost a gentleman, sprang toward the entrance door and disappeared down the stairway.

I sat down again. This was becoming interesting. I waited for the husband, who was a long
time getting the wine. At length I heard him coming
upstairs, and the sound of his steps made me laugh,
one of those solitary laughs which one cannot re-
strain.

He came in, bringing two bottles, and asked:

" Is my wife still asleep? You have not heard
her moving about? "

I suspected that she had her ear to the door,
and I said:

" No, I have heard nothing."

And now he again called out:

" Pauline! "

She made no reply, and did not even move.

He came back to me, and explained:

" You see, she doesn't like me to come home at
night and take a drop with a friend."

" So you think she is not asleep? "

" Of course she is not asleep." He seemed annoyed.

" Well, at any rate," he said, " let us have a
drink together."

And he at once showed a disposition to empty
the two bottles, one after the other, without more
ado.

This time I did display some energy. When I
had swallowed one glass I rose up to leave. He no
longer spoke of accompanying me, and, glancing
toward his wife's door with a sullen scowl, the scowl
of a common man in an angry mood, the scowl of
a brute whose violence is only slumbering, he muttered:

" She'll have to open that door when you are
gone."

I stared at this poltroon, who had worked himself into a fit of rage without knowing why, perhaps
owing to an obscure presentiment, the instinct of the
deceived male who does not like closed doors. He
had talked about her to me in a tender strain; now
assuredly he was going to beat her.

He exclaimed, as he shook the lock once more:

" Pauline! "

A voice like that of a woman waking out of her sleep replied from behind the partition:

" Eh! What? "

" Didn't you hear me come in? "

" No, I was asleep! Let me rest. "

" Open the door! "

" Yes, when you're alone. I don't like you to be bringing home fellows at night to drink with you. "

Then I took myself off, stumbling down the stairs, just as the other man had done, whose accomplice I was. And, as I resumed my journey toward Paris, I realized that I had just witnessed in this wretched abode a scene of the eternal drama which is being enacted every day, in every form, and in every class, and in every hemisphere.

# A Philosopher

I HAD no secrets from Blérot, who had been my intimate friend from childhood. We were united heart and soul, like brothers, and were mutual confidants of each other's love affairs.

When he told me that he was going to get married I felt hurt, as if he had been guilty of treachery toward me. I felt that it must interfere with that cordial and absolute affection which had united us hitherto. His wife would come between us. The intimacy of marriage establishes a kind of complicity of mysterious alliance between two persons, even when they have ceased to love each other. Man and wife are like two discreet partners who will not let any one else into their secrets. But that close bond which the conjugal kiss rivets is widely loosened on the day on which the woman takes a lover.

I remember Blérot's wedding as if it were but yesterday. I would not be present at the signing of the marriage contract, as I have no

particular liking for such ceremonies, but I only
went to the civil wedding and to the church.

His wife, whom I had never seen before, was a
tall, slight girl, with pale hair, pale cheeks, pale
hands, and eyes to match. She walked with a
slightly undulating motion, as if she were on board
a ship, and seemed to advance with a succession of
long, graceful curtsies.

Blérot seemed very much in love with her. He
looked at her constantly, and I felt a shiver of im-
moderate desire for her pass through my frame.

I went to see him a few days after the wedding,
and he said to me:

" You do not know how happy I am; I am madly
in love with her; but then she is  .  .  .  she is.
.  .  ." He did not finish his sentence, but he put
the tips of his fingers to his lips with a gesture
which signified:

" Divine! delicious! perfect! " and a good deal
more besides.

I asked, laughing: " What! All that? "

" Everything that you can imagine," was his
answer.

He introduced me to her. She was very pleasant, on easy terms with me, as was natural, and
begged me to look upon their house as my own. I
felt that he, Blérot, did not belong to me any longer.
Our intimacy was altogether checked, and we hardly
found a word to say to each other.

I soon took my leave, and shortly afterward went
to the East, and returned by way of Russia, Ger-
many, Sweden, and Holland, after an absence of
eighteen months from Paris.

The morning after my arrival, as I was walking along the boulevards to breathe the air of my

native city once more, I saw a pale man with sunken
cheeks coming toward me, who was as much like
Blérot as it was possible for a physically emaciated
man to be to a strong, ruddy, rather stout man. I
looked at him in surprise, and asked myself: "Can
it possibly be he?" But he saw me, and came toward me with outstretched arms, and we embraced
in the middle of the boulevard.

After we had gone up and down once or twice
from the Rue Drouot to the Vaudeville Theater, as
we were taking leave of each other, I said to him:

"You don't look at all well. Are you ill?"

"I do feel rather out of sorts," was all he said.

He looked like a man who was going to die, and
I felt a flood of affection for my old friend, the only
real friend I had ever had. · I squeezed his hands.

"What is the matter with you? Are you in
pain?"

"A little tired; but it is nothing."

"What does your doctor say?"

"He calls it anæmia, and has ordered me to eat
no white meat and to take tincture of iron."

A suspicion flashed across me.

"Are you happy?" I asked him.

"Yes, very happy; my wife is charming, and I
love her more than ever."

But I noticed that he grew rather red and
seemed embarrassed, as if he were afraid of any
further questions, so I took him by the arm and
pushed him into a café, which was nearly empty at
that time of day. I forced him to sit down, and,
looking him straight in the face, I said:

"Look here, old fellow, just tell me the exact
truth."

"I have nothing to tell you," he stammered.

"That is not true," I replied firmly. "You are ill, mentally perhaps, and you dare not reveal your secret to any one. Something or other is injuring your health, and I mean you to tell me what it is. Come, I am waiting for you to begin."

Again he got very red, stammered, and, turning his head away, said:

"It is very idiotic—but I—I am done for!"

As he did not go on, I said:

"Just tell me what it is."

"Well, it is my wife—that is all," he said abruptly, almost desperately.

I did not understand at first. "Does she make you unhappy? How? What is it?"

"No," he replied, in a low voice, as if he were confessing some crime; "I love her too much, that is all."

I was thunderstruck at this brutal avowal, and then I felt inclined to laugh, but at length managed to reply:

"But surely, at least so it seems to me, you might manage to—to love her a little less."

He had grown very pale again, and at length made up his mind to speak to me frankly, as he used to do formerly.

"No," he said, "that is impossible; and I am dying from it, I know; it is killing me, and I am really frightened. Some days, like to-day, I feel inclined to leave her, to go away altogether, to start for the other end of the world, so as to live for a long time; and then, when the evening comes, I return home in spite of myself, but slowly, and feeling uncomfortable. I go upstairs hesitatingly and ring, and when I go in I see her there sitting in her easy-chair, and she says: 'How late you are!' I kiss her, and we sit down to dinner. During the meal I think to myself: 'I will go directly it is over, and take the train for somewhere, no matter where;' but when we get back to the drawing-room I am so tired that I have not the courage to get up out of my chair, and so I remain, and then—and then—I succumb again.''

I could not help smiling again. He saw it, and said: "You may laugh, but I assure you it is very horrible."

"Why don't you tell your wife?" I asked him. "Unless she be a regular monster she would understand."

He shrugged his shoulders. "It is all very well for you to talk. I don't tell her because I know her nature. Have you ever heard it said of certain women, 'She has just married a third time?' Well, that makes you laugh as you did just now, and yet it is true. What is to be done? It is neither her fault nor mine. She is so because nature has made her so; I assure you, my dear old friend, she has the temperament of a Messalina. She does not know it, but I do; so much the worse for me. She seems like an ignorant schoolgirl, and she really is ignorant, poor child.

"Every day I form energetic resolutions, for you must understand that I am dying. But one look of her eyes, one of those looks in which I can read the ardent desire of her lips, is enough for me, and I succumb at once, saying to myself: 'This is really the end; I will have no more of her death-giving kisses,' and then, when I have yielded again, as I have to-day, I go out and walk on ahead, thinking of death, and saying to myself that I am lost, that all is over.

" I am so mentally ill that I went for a walk to
Père Lachaise cemetery yesterday. I looked at
all the graves, standing in a row like dominoes, and
thought to myself: ' I shall soon be there,' and then
I returned home, quite determined to pretend to be
ill, and so escape, but I could not.

" Oh! You don't know what it is. Ask a
smoker who is poisoning himself with nicotine
whether he can give up his delicious and deadly
habit. He will tell you that he has tried a hundred times without success, and he will, perhaps,
add: ' More's the pity, but I had rather die than
go without tobacco.' That is just the case with me.
When once one is in the clutches of such a passion
or such a vice, one gives one's self up to it entirely."

He got up and gave me his hand. I was seized
with a tumult of rage, and with hatred for this
woman, this careless, charming, terrible woman; and
as Blérot was buttoning up his coat to go out I said
to him, brutally perhaps:

" But, in God's name, why don't you let her
have a lover, rather than kill yourself like that? "

He shrugged his shoulders without replying, and
went off.

For six months I did not see him. Every morning I expected a letter of invitation to his funeral,
but would not go to his house from a complicated
feeling of contempt for him and for that woman,
a feeling of anger, indignation, of a thousand sensations.

One lovely spring morning I was walking in the
Champs Elysées. It was one of those warm days
which make our eyes bright and stir in us a tumul-
tuous feeling of happiness from the mere sense of
existence. Some one tapped me on the shoulder,

and, turning round, I saw my old friend, looking
well, stout, and rosy.

He gave me both hands, beaming with pleasure,
and exclaimed:

"Here you are, you erratic individual!"

I looked at him, utterly thunderstruck.

"Well, on my word—yes. By Jove! I congratulate you; you have indeed changed in the last
six months!"

He flushed scarlet, and said, with an embarrassed
laugh:

"One can but do one's best."

I looked at him so persistently that he evidently
felt uncomfortable, and I went on:

"So—now—you are—completely cured?"

He stammered, hastily:

"Yes, perfectly, thank you." Then, changing
his tone: "How lucky that I should have come
across you, old fellow! I hope we shall often meet
now."

But I would not give up my idea; I wanted to
know how matters really stood, and I asked:

"Don't you remember what you told me six
months ago? I suppose—I—eh—suppose you control yourself now?"

"Please don't talk any more about it," he replied uneasily; "forget that I mentioned it to you.
But I have no intention of letting you go; you must
come and dine at my house."

A sudden fancy took me to see for myself how
matters stood, so that I might understand all about
it, and I accepted.

His wife received me in a most charming manner, and she was, in fact, a most attractive woman.
Her long hands and her neck and cheeks were beau-

tifully white and delicate, and marked her breeding, and her walk was undulating and delightful.

René gave her a brotherly kiss on the forehead
and said:

" Has not Lucien come yet? "

" Not yet," she replied, in a clear, soft voice;
" you know he is almost always rather late."

At that moment the bell rang, and a tall man was
shown in. He was dark, with a thick beard, and
looked like a modern Hercules. We were introduced
to each other; his name was Lucien Delabarre.

René and he shook hands in a most friendly manner, and then we went to dinner.

It was a most enjoyable meal, without the least
constraint. My old friend spoke with me constantly, in the old familiar, cordial manner, just as
he used to do. It was: "You know, old fellow! "
" I say, old fellow! " " Just listen a moment, old
fellow! " Suddenly he exclaimed:

" You don't know how glad I am to see you
again; it takes me back to old times."

I looked at his wife and the other man. Their
attitude was perfectly correct, though I fancied once
or twice that they exchanged a rapid and furtive
glance.

As soon as dinner was over René turned to his
wife, and said:

" My dear, I have just met Pierre again, and I
am going to carry him off for a walk and a chat
along the boulevards to remind us of old times. I
am leaving you in very good company."

The young woman smiled, and said to me, as
she shook hands with me:

" Don't keep him too long."

As we went along, arm in arm, I could not help

saying to him, for I was determined to know how matters stood:

" I say, what has happened? Do tell me! "

He, however, interrupted me roughly, and answered like a man who has been disturbed without any reason.

" Just look here, old fellow; let a man alone with your questions."

Then he added, half aloud, as if talking to himself:

" After all, it would have been too stupid to have let one's self be killed like that."

I did not press him. We walked on quickly and began to talk. All of a sudden he whispered in my ear:

" I say, suppose we go and have a bottle of ' fizz ' with some girls! Eh? "

I could not prevent myself from laughing heartily.

" Just as you like; come along, let us go."

# What Was the Matter With Andrew

THE lawyer's house looked out on the square. Behind it there was a well-kept garden, with a back entrance into a narrow street which was almost always deserted, and from which it was separated by a wall.

At the bottom of that garden Maître Moreau's wife had promised, for the first time, to meet Captain Sommerive, who had been making love to her for a long time.

Her husband had gone to Paris for a week, so she was quite free for the time being. The Captain had begged so hard, and had used such loving words; she was certain that he loved her ardently, and she felt so isolated, so misunderstood, so neglected amid all the law business which seemed to be her husband's sole pleasure, that she had given away her heart without even asking herself whether it would give her anything else at some future time.

Then, after some months of platonic love, of pressing of hands, of kisses rapidly stolen behind a door, the Captain had declared that he would ask

permission to exchange, and leave the town immediately, if she would not grant him a meeting, a real meeting, during her husband's absence; and so at length she yielded to his importunity.

Just then she was waiting, close against the wall, with a beating heart, trembling at the slightest sound, and when at last she heard somebody climbing up the wall, she very nearly ran away, but controlled herself and stayed.

Suppose it were not he, but a thief? But no; some one called out softly, " Matilda! " and when she replied, "Etienne!" a man jumped on to the path with a crash.

It was he—and what a kiss!

For a long time they remained in each other's arms. But suddenly a fine rain began to fall, and the drops from the leaves fell on her neck and made her start. Whereupon he said:

"Matilda, my adored one, my darling, my angel, let us go indoors. It is twelve o'clock; we can have nothing to fear."

"No, dearest; I am too frightened."

But he held her in his arms, and whispered in her ear:

"Your servants sleep on the third floor, looking out on the square, and your room, on the first, looks on to the garden, so nobody can hear us. I love you so that I wish to love you entirely, from head to foot." And he kissed her fervently.

She resisted still, frightened and even ashamed. But he put his arms round her, lifted her up, and carried her out of the rain, which was by this time descending in torrents.

The door was open; they groped their way upstairs, and when they were in the room he bolted the door while she lit a match.

Then she fell, half fainting, into a chair, while he knelt down beside her.

At last she said, panting:

"No! no! Etienne, please let me remain a virtuous woman. This is so horrid, so common. Cannot we love each other with a spiritual love only? . . . Oh! Etienne!"

But he was beyond reasoning with, and she got up and tried to escape him, by hiding behind the curtains of the bedstead. As he hastily followed her his belt, which was loose, slipped off and his sword fell to the floor with a crash.

A prolonged, shrill infant's cry came from the next room, the door of which had remained open.

" You have awakened the child," she whispered, " and perhaps he will not go to sleep again."

He was only fifteen months old, and slept in a room opening out of hers, so that she might be able to hear him.

The Captain exclaimed ardently:

" What does it matter, Matilda? How I love you! Come to me, Matilda."

But she struggled, and resisted in her fright.

" No! no! Just listen how he is crying; he will wake up the nurse, and what should we do if she were to come? We should be lost. Just listen to me, Etienne. When he screams at night his father always takes him into our bed, and he is quiet immediately; it is the only means of keeping him still. Do let me take him. . . ."

The child roared, uttered shrill screams, which pierced the thickest walls, so as to be heard by passers-by in the streets.

In his consternation, Etienne allowed her to go and get the child, which she brought in and placed on the bed, when he was quiet at once.

Etienne sat astride a chair and made a cigarette, and in five minutes Andrew went to sleep again.

" I will take him back," his mother said; and she took him back very carefully to his bed.

When she returned, the Captain was waiting for her with open arms, and put his arms round her in a transport of love, while she said, stammering:

" Oh! Etienne, my darling, if you only knew how I love you; how . . ."

Andrew began to cry again, and he, in a rage, exclaimed:

"Confound it all, won't the little brute be quiet?"

No, the little brute would not be quiet, but, on the contrary, howled all the louder.

Matilda thought she heard a noise downstairs; no doubt the nurse was coming, so she jumped up and took the child into bed, and he grew quiet directly.

Three times she put him back, and three times she had to fetch him again, and an hour before daybreak the Captain had to go, swearing like the proverbial trooper; and, to calm his impatience, Matilda said he might come again the next night.

Of course he came, more impatient and ardent than ever, excited by the delay.

He took care to put his sword carefully into a corner; he took off his boots like a thief, and spoke so low that Matilda could hardly hear him. But just as he thought all was quiet a cry, feeble at first, but which grew louder every moment, made itself heard. Andrew was awake again.

He uttered little spasmodic wails, and there was not the slightest doubt that if he went on like that the whole house would awake; so his mother, not knowing what to do, went and brought him in. The Captain was more furious than ever, but did not move, and very carefully he put out his hand, took a small piece of the child's skin between his two fingers, no matter where it was, the thighs or elsewhere, and pinched it. The little one struggled and screamed in a deafening manner, but his tormentor pinched everywhere furiously and more vigorously. He took a morsel of flesh and twisted and turned it,

and then let go in order to take hold of another
piece, and then another and another.

The child screamed like a chicken that is having
its throat cut, or a dog that is being mercilessly
beaten.  His mother caressed him, kissed him, and
tried to stifle his cries by her tenderness; but Andrew grew purple, as if he were going into convul-
sions, and kicked and struggled with his little arms
and legs in an alarming manner.

The Captain said softly:

" Try and take him back to his cradle; perhaps
he will be quiet."

And Matilda went into the other room with the
child in her arms.

As soon as he was out of his mother's bed he
cried less loudly, and when he was in his own he was
quiet, with the exception of a few broken sobs.

The rest of the night was tranquil.

The next night Etienne came again.  As he happened to speak rather loudly, Andrew awoke again
and began to scream.  His mother went and fetched
him immediately, but the Captain pinched so hard
and long that the child was nearly suffocated by its
cries, and its eyes turned in its head and it foamed
at the mouth; as soon as it was back in its cradle
it was quiet, and in four days Andrew did not cry
any more to come into his mother's bed.

On Saturday evening the lawyer returned and
took his place again at the domestic hearth.

As he was tired with his journey he went to bed
early; but he had not long lain down when he said
to his wife:

" Why, how is it that Andrew is not crying?
Just go and fetch him, Matilda; I like to feel that he
is between us."

She got up and brought the child, but as soon
as he saw that he was in that bed, in which he had
been so fond of sleeping a few days previously, he
wriggled and screamed so violently in his fright
that she had to take him back to his cradle.

M. Moreau could not get over his surprise.
"What a very funny thing! What is the matter
with him this evening? I suppose he is sleepy?"

"He has been like that all the time that you
were away; I have never been able to have him in
bed with me once."

In the morning the child woke up and began to
laugh and play with his toys.

The lawyer, who was an affectionate man, got
up, kissed his offspring, and took him into his arms
to carry him to their bed. Andrew laughed, with
the vacant laugh of little creatures whose ideas are
still vague. He suddenly saw the bed and his
mother in it, and his happy little face puckered up,
till suddenly he began to scream furiously, and
struggled as if he were going to be put to the torture.

In his astonishment his father said:

"There must be something the matter with the
child," and mechanically he lifted up his little night-
shirt.

He uttered a prolonged "O—o—h!" of astonishment. The child's calves, thighs, and legs were
covered with blue spots as big as halfpennies.

"Just look, Matilda!" the father exclaimed;
"this is horrible!" And the mother rushed forward in a fright. It was horrible; no doubt the beginning of some sort of leprosy, of one of those
strange affections of the skin which doctors are
often at a loss to account for.

The parents looked at one another in consternation.

"We must send for the doctor," the father said.

But Matilda, pale as death, was looking at her child, who was spotted like a leopard. Then, suddenly uttering a violent cry as if she had seen something that filled her with horror, she exclaimed:

"Oh! the wretch!"

In his astonishment M. Moreau asked: "What are you talking about? What wretch?"

She got red up to the roots of her hair, and stammered:

"Oh, nothing! but I think I can guess—it must be—we ought to send for the doctor . . . it must be that wretch of a nurse who has been pinching the poor child to make him keep quiet when he cries."

In his rage the lawyer sent for the nurse, and very nearly beat her. She denied it most impudently, but was instantly dismissed, and the Municipality having been informed of her conduct, she will find it a hard matter to get another situation.